Tales of The Scary Queen Vol: 1

A.M. Burns

ACKNOWLEDGMENTS

Thanks to the Tuesday Writers Group for all their input and my awesome beta readers for their hard work.
And as always, thanks to my wonderfully supportive and funny husband Jay for the inspiration for the book.

1
Rocky Road

Conrad Bale stared at the glass door with trepidation. The stress of unemployment weighed heavily on him. Since leaving the Air Force nine months earlier, he'd scoured Dallas looking for a job. Everywhere he went, he was either underqualified or overqualified. No one understood he was willing to try, and having a job was more important than anything. He'd recently received his last unemployment check. His mother assured him he'd always have a room in her basement, but he wanted more.

The "help wanted" sign in the window taunted him. He stared at the bright green logo painted on the window. *Is this really the last place in town I haven't put in a job application?* Conrad looked at his watch, thirteen-thirteen. The lunch crowd had died down a quarter of an hour ago. He shifted the messenger bag on his shoulder, sighed and reached for the door handle.

A loud clank sounded as the door closed behind him. Conrad glanced back, startled by the sound. A heavy antique cowbell hung from the door. The clean, white marble floor squeaked under his loafers. He tried to remember if he'd walked through a puddle and gotten his soles wet. The smell of waffle cones hit him as a door behind the counter swung opened. The figure that emerged was crowned by well-teased black hair.

"Welcome to Scary Queen. How may I help you?" a deep voice flowed from garish red lips on a lined face that no amount of makeup could improve.

Conrad resisted the urge to turn around and leave. He'd been in the little ice-cream shop before, but couldn't recall ever encountering this particular person. *Do I need a job so badly I could work in this place?* He squared his shoulders and ran a hand through his short mouse-brown hair. *I probably won't get hired anyway, but I have to try.*

"I saw your help wanted sign and wanted to apply." Conrad tried not to sound nervous.

The androgynous, yet somehow female worker broke into a wide grin. "Well, why didn't you say so?" With quick steps, *she* pranced over to the antique cash register. Seconds later her well-manicured, talon-like hand passed a job application to him. "Do you need a pen?" *she* asked in a gravelly voice.

"No, I have one." Conrad resisted the urge to snatch the application away from the woman.

"Have a seat over there," she gestured to one of the small square tables near the window that looked out onto Cedar Springs. "Would you care for something to drink while you fill it out?"

Conrad swallowed. He hadn't realized he was thirsty. "Sure. Any soda will be fine, I'm easy."

"We hope so." Her lined face cracked a smile again as the server turned, swished the black dress and strutted toward the soda fountain.

5

Conrad walked over to the table closest to the door, hung his messenger bag over the back of the small café chair, extracted a pen, sat, and started filling in the application. Right after he'd written his name on the form, the shopkeeper showed up with his drink.

"If you need anything ring the bell on the counter," she said. "I'll be in the back."

"Thanks." Conrad accepted the cold glass. He tried not to watch her narrow hips as she swished the heel-length black lace dress back through the door behind the counter, but it had the appeal of a train wreck. He took a long draw from the soda, then turned his attention back to the application.

***

"Shoppe likes him," Scoop said in a soft voice as Dracanna closed the door to the front of the shop.

"What do you mean?" She walked over to the sink brimming with soap suds and dishes.

"The bell clanked when he came in and the floor squeaked."

"It's a bell, it's supposed to clank," Dracanna snarled.

"When was the last time that bell clanked?"

"You know, I could just kill Bobi Sox for picking today to walk out!" Dracanna grumbled, ignoring the question.

"Shoppe didn't like her," the voice replied. "She had to go."

"But on the same day Lilly called in sick?" With a sharp snap, Dracanna pulled on a pair of pink rubber gloves. "I'm tired of being short-staffed at inopportune times."

"Then go out there and hire him. Maybe he can start right now."

Dracanna snatched up the ice-cream scoop that lay on

the counter. She glared at it. "Like we have anything in his size just lying around," she shrieked at the metal instrument. "He's right down the middle, everything we have in the back will either be too large or too small for him."

The ice-cream scoop chuckled. "So, send him down to the Salvation Army. We're in Dallas, right? If I recall correctly, they're just a couple blocks over."

With pink-gloved hands, she plunged the ice cream scoop into the hot soapy water. "We'll see what his application looks like before we hire him."

Dracanna swiped a heavy yellow celluloid sponge across a bit of clinging ice cream away from the edge of the scoop.

"Hey, no need to get nasty about things," Scoop complained. "I thought I told you to go get some real sponges to use on me, not this synthetic crap."

"Let me run the shop the way I see fit," Dracanna replied.

"I thought we were a team."

Dracanna passed Scoop under warm water to rinse off the remaining soap. "We are. But remember, when dealing with humans, I have the last word, not you or Shoppe."

A package of sugar fell off a nearby shelf, landed with a loud thud, and split open sending white granules flying around the back room. Dracanna glared at the ceiling and sighed.

"Sometimes, I wish I could just burn this place to the ground." She laid the metal scoop down loud enough it clanged on the steel counter, yanked off the pink gloves, snatched up the nearby broom and set to work cleaning up the sugar. "If I did figure out a way to burn it down, who knows what implications that would cause in the universe, not to mention my pocketbook."

As Dracanna dumped the last of the ruined sugar in the large trashcan by the back door, the little bell on the front counter rang.

***

Conrad stared at the third page of the application. The last two lines were asking for his first childhood pet's name and the name of the street he lived on when he went to school. They'd moved around a lot, so he couldn't remember the name of the street. He still recalled the little terrier they'd had when he was growing up. *Rex. But why do they need that? Maybe it's for the computer password or something.* He jotted down Harrison for the street and then double checked all the other information to make sure it was correct.

By the time he verified he'd dotted all the I's and crossed all the T's, the shopkeeper in the black dress still hadn't returned. Conrad walked over to the counter. The small silver bell gave a short high-pitched ring as he struck it.

"Just a minute," the now-familiar, gravelly voice called out from the back room.

As he waited, Conrad perused the ice cream display. He wondered what Rainbow Licorice tasted like. It was certainly brightly colored, but Pinky Pie just didn't sound appetizing. The name and the strange putrid pink color made him wrinkle his nose.

"Ah, you're finished," the storekeeper said, coming through the door.

Conrad jerked up at the rough sound of the voice. The black dress looked a little worse than it had a few minutes before. The edge of the long dress was wrinkled and sparkly, like she'd spilled something on it.

"Yes, got it all done." Conrad held up the completed

8

application.

"Well, let's sit down and look it over, shall we?"

They walked over to the small table where Conrad had filled out the form moments before. His messenger bag was still there, and the partially consumed soda. Her craggy hand with its well-manicured, dark-blue nails moved rapidly across the lines of information.

"So, it looks like you've worked in food service a few years back." Her ageless black eyes looked up from the paper to peer into Conrad's. "Why are you looking to rejoin the food service industry, Conrad? You were military."

Conrad swallowed under the intensity of the dark gaze. "I've always enjoyed working with people, sir."

The shopkeeper reared back like she'd been slapped. Conrad's heart stopped at the look of horror on the heavily-caked face.

"You *will* refer to me as *Madame!*" Her voice took on an inhuman pitch Conrad had never heard before. "I'll have you know that everything's been changed but the *voice!*"

Conrad felt the blood flow out of his face. "I'm so sorry," he stammered, grabbed the strap of his bag and moved to get out of his seat. "Perhaps I should leave."

"Stay!" The glare intensified as she pointed a crooked finger at him. "We're not done here. So you like working with people?"

Conrad settled back into the hard metal chair. "Yes ma'am. I actually missed working with people. My military career was a desk job, mostly paperwork, and high stress."

"I can't say things don't get stressful around here, from time to time." She continued to look over the application. "So tell me, why I should give you the job and not the next skinny little twink who walks through the door?"

"Well," Conrad tried to think of the right thing to say. He needed the job, even if the boss was some kind of odd transsexual who looked like she was straight off the ship from *Transylvania*. "I live close by."

"Sweetie, so does every other little boi who comes in here."

Conrad gulped. "I've got experience."

"Five years ago, at Baskin Robbins, I'll give you that much."

"I'm a hard worker, and like to keep my jobs."

Her blue nails tapped on the ceramic tile table top. The grout in between the tiles was almost the same color as the nail polish. "So why don't you have one now?"

"No one is hiring ex-military right now. They're all afraid of PTSD. "

"And how do you look in a dress?"

Conrad paused.

Seconds ticked by. A trickle of sweat ran down his back.

He tried to decide what to say. *I've never worn a dress. I'd have to wear a dress to work here?* "How do I look in a what?"

"A dress, dearie. How do you look in a dress?" She gestured to her own ensemble. "This is a themed establishment. People come in to see bois in dresses. I mean, our ice cream is some of the best you'll find anywhere, but people come in for the staff spectacle. If I could get away with it, I'd have a bunch of little muscle twinks in Speedos serving, but the health department wouldn't go for it, and what would I call the place then, Hunky Cream? It just doesn't have the same ring to it as Scary Queen." Her black gaze returned to Conrad. "So, how do you look in a dress?"

"I don't really know."

10

The shopkeeper was silent for a moment while her ageless eyes stared at Conrad. The gaze was almost like that of someone undressing him, but somehow he thought she was actually playing mental dress up instead.

Finally, she placed a finger on her narrow chin and nodded. "I think you'll look just fine."

Am I happy or terrified? The job will bring much needed money, and I'll do anything for money right now. Well, almost anything. I'm not ready to make a living on my back, like Freddie from the bar suggested a couple weeks ago. But working in a dress will be really awkward.

She turned to the final page of the application. "No, no, no…this will never do." Not a single black hair moved as she shook her heavily- hair-sprayed head.

"What's wrong?" Conrad heard his future finances run screaming out the door.

"We'll have to come up with a better name than this."

"What's wrong with Conrad?"

"Not Conrad, silly." A frown lined her craggy face even more. "Rex Harrison. Sorry, too butch. We need a proper drag name for you. You're replacing Bobi Sox. His real name was Robert Shoe. Now, let me think."

"Does this mean I have the job?"

"If we can come up a good name for you, and if you can find proper attire by this evening."

"You want me to start this evening?"

"The sooner the better," she replied. "I had a girl quit on me this morning after another called in sick, and I'm short-staffed. I handled the lunch crowd on my own. One gal's coming in around four, but we'll be short unless you can show up. We normally need three to four of us to handle the after-dinner and bar crowd. We don't close until three in the morning."

"So what do I wear?"

"Today's a normal day." She messaged her narrow chin with her scrawny hand. "By any chance, are you about the same size as your mother?"

Conrad's mom was the same height as he, but she was a bit heavier. "Yeah, I might be able to get something from her. Will I need anything else? What about a wig? My mother doesn't have a wig."

"Wigs I have. Medium sized clothes…not so much. Run home, get your mama's dress and when you get back here, we'll see what we can do to fix you up a bit. Don't worry about high heels or anything overly uncomfortable for your feet. We tend to dress down below the ankles."

The prospect of being gainfully employed made Conrad's heart soar. "Thank you…ma'am." He reached out his hand to the woman.

"You can call me Dracanna," she said as her dainty clawed hand closed on Conrad's. A shiver ran up his arm as their skin touched.

"Thank you, Dracanna," Conrad said as he stood to leave. "I'll be back as soon as I can…within the hour."

"That would be good. Try and think of a drag name for yourself while you're gone."

***

The cowbell clanked again as Conrad left. Dracanna frowned while she continued to sit at the table. She recognized the tone of the clank this time. *Shoppe does like the new boy. What does that mean in the big scheme of things? It's been a long time since Shoppe liked someone enough to clang the bell in that particular tone. The last one was that guy in Las Vegas, went by the name Paula Pecs, and we lost him in the freezer after a year.*

Dracanna rose, brushed more of the sugar off her

12

black dress and went to finish the rest of the lunch dishes. *There's no way to avoid hashing this out with Scoop. That obnoxious implement is probably back there ready to start shooting campy names for the boy at me as soon as I walk through the door. At least I've got a nearly-full crew again. But how long will that last?*

***

"Are you sure about this job, Conrad?" his mother asked. Hangers clanked as she dug through her closet for something suitable.

"It's a job, Mom." He held up a dress with a plunging neckline. "Not a career. It'll hold me over till something better comes along." He handed the dress back to her.

"What's wrong with that one?" she asked, looking at the red velvet.

"The neckline's too low. I'd have to shave my chest, and we don't have that much time. I told him…I mean her, that I'd be back within the hour."

"Here, try this." She handed him a blue gingham dress with short billowy sleeves.

"Mom, I'd look like a milk maid."

"But it has a high neckline, and you *are* working in an ice cream shop."

Conrad sighed. "Fine, do you have a belt that would go with it?"

She threw out a wide leather belt. "This might work. Are you really sure about this? I mean think about it, what are the guys going to say about you wearing a dress? And an ice cream shop again. Remember the last time, before you joined the Air Force, you put on so much weight."

"Mom, this place is in the heart of Gay Dallas." He laid the belt against the gingham dress. *I guess this will work.* "It's not like it's in the Galleria or something. Folks

13

won't care. According to Dracanna people come in to see the guys in dresses. If any of my friends have a problem with it, then they weren't really my friends were they. Besides, I need the money. With all the outsourcing and everything, I can't get any kind of job, and even if I go back to college on a military aid grant, there's still basic bills to be paid. This is better than nothing, and it'll give me time to figure out what I want to do with my life."

His mother sighed and closed her closet door. "I just worry about you. You're my only son."

Conrad picked up the dress and the belt. He flashed her a big smile. "Well, maybe you can start thinking of me as your only daughter now."

She frowned at him.

"Hey, if nothing else, maybe I can meet a cute guy there. There will be a ton coming in every day." *That might be nice, find a boyfriend while I'm making some cash. Life is sure to pick up.*

***

The bell clanged again as Conrad entered Scary Queen. The tile floor squeaked under his tennis shoes as he scanned about for Dracanna.

"Be there in a minute," Dracanna's gravelly voice called out from the back.

"It's me, Conrad," he called.

"Oh, come into the back."

Conrad pushed through the door behind the counter. He looked around the room, which was bigger than he expected, trying to find his new boss.

"Oh dear Goddess, look what the tornado just dropped in our store!" a new voice exclaimed from across the room. "Bitch, you better watch out for falling houses. I know I'm safe, but you."

A pair of broad shoulders clad in a clingy chiffon dress walked toward Conrad. Under the bangs of a bright red wig, large blue eyes, more male than female, peered at him. He resisted the urge to step back from the person.

"Hi, I thought I heard Dracanna back here," Conrad replied, cautiously closing the door.

"Over here," Dracanna's gravelly voice replied from behind the door. She sat working at a desk that had been blocked from Conrad's view. "So, say hello to Bea Mann. You'll be working with her tonight. She came in early to help out. Bea, this is Conrad. We haven't come up with a working name yet."

"Oh, honey," the big redhead said as she hung pink rubber gloves on the sink. "He also needs a wig and some boobs. That dress just screams for a big set of corn-fed, Dolly Parton boobs."

Dracanna waved a hand toward another door. "Go into the dressing room and finish getting him done up. Conrad, did you think of a name?"

"No ma'am, I didn't"

Bea laughed. "'No ma'am, I didn't?' Aren't you just precious? In a couple of days you'll call her Bitch, just like the rest of us."

Dracanna shot Bea a sideways glare. "As you can see, we're a familiar bunch around here."

"Oh, don't mind her," Bea said, gesturing for Conrad to follow. "She worked the lunch rush by herself, thanks to Bobi. That lazy bitch never liked this place anyway. Come on, let's get you finished out."

They walked through the next door into a room that had racks and shelves full of all sorts of clothes, wigs and other accoutrements that reminded Conrad of theater dressing room scenes he'd seen in movies. *I can't believe that they wouldn't have anything back here that would fit me. Well Dracanna had said something about everything was either too large or too small.* Bea pushed him down into a barber's chair in front of the closer of two mirrors in the room.

"I bet you've never put on makeup before either," Bea smiled. "Otherwise you'd have come with your own wig. Well, we have plenty of both back here. Help yourself until you can afford your own. Some of these are things others have left behind. Dracanna has them cleaned, but you never know what's lurking in the seams… if you know what I mean."

Conrad looked at himself in the mirror as Bea went digging through a pile of boxes next to the station. Suddenly, she held up a foam head with a short brown wig cut in a bob. "Here, I think this will look fabulous on you. It might even fit."

"What do you mean fit?" Conrad asked, looking at the mass of brown hair. "It's a wig. They have sizes?"

"Of course they do! This one's a large. Miz Thang out front used to wear a petite until her own hair grew out." Bea stood behind Conrad and settled the wig onto his head. It felt strange and awkward, almost like a skullcap, but airier and hairier. Staring in the mirror, Conrad watched in stunned silence. Bea's large hands tugged and fluffed for several minutes before she looked satisfied.

"Oh, definitely. And this goes so well with the dress, gives you a certain Mary Ann look, you know … from Gilligan's Island."

Bea tortured him for nearly half an hour with the makeup and gel packs, getting everything just right. "That's about all I can do." Bea patted Conrad's head. "Considering you make a much better Brad than you do an Angelina, I

16

think I did a great job. Now let's go see what her Bitchiness thinks."

Dracanna walked through the door from the front as they emerged.

"Ta *Da…*" Bea gestured dramatically around Conrad. "What do you think?"

With dark eyes scowling, Dracanna gave a heavy sigh through her too-thin red lips. "I think she looks like Dolly Parton getting ready to go milk the cows. Why on earth did you put four gel packs on her?"

"The dress is a little big on her and we needed to fill it out," Bea explained.

Dracanna shook her dark head slowly. "You should've taken some of the dress up in the back."

"Hey, she's serving ice cream, it won't matter."

Dracanna glared. "Did you think of a name?"

"Bea likes Cat Astrophe," Conrad spoke up. He kind of liked the name too. It fit the way the job felt to him.

Rolling her eyes, Dracanna emitted another long, dramatic sigh. "It's been that sort of a day. It works for now. Bea, before we get busy, show *Cat* around. Explain how we do things. And don't *forget to warn* her about the *freezers*."

***

"Cat Astrophe, I like it." Scoop said after the door closed on Cat and Bea.

"You would," Dracanna snapped. She marched over to the ice cream scoop and snatched it up from the special holder where it sat when not in use. "Now, would you care to tell me why he's important to Shoppe?"

"I have no idea," the implement replied. "And after your little comment earlier about burning down the place, Shoppe isn't talking."

"Well, I just hope her working name *is* ironic in every

way, shape and form."

***

"Okay, stocking is the easy part," Bea explained as they stopped in front of the freezers, just the other side of the ice cream counter. "All the tubs go in either freezer one or freezer two. They're alphabetical. If you run out of something, come over, find fresh one and put it into the correct spot in the display. If we're out of it in the freezer—" She scanned through the tubs sitting there on the metal shelves. "Yeah, looks like we're out of Quick Kiwi—you go around back, find it in the big freezer, and put another one in from the back." She turned to the next freezer. "Now freezer three, this one you only stock from the front. We have a special…system with this freezer. It's where the customers can pull out cakes, ice-cream sandwiches or other pre-made things."

Conrad looked in at the brightly-decorated, chilled cakes. "But if the customers are getting things out of there wouldn't it be easier to load it from the back?"

Bea shuddered and for a moment her voice drop to a masculine tone. "Trust me kid, you really don't want to open the back of that freezer."

"So, on over here," Bea led Conrad away from the freezers over to the ice-cream counter as the front door opened and their first customer of the evening entered the store.

***

Several hours later, Conrad plopped down in the barber chair in front of the mirror. Dracanna insisted that he take a lunch break during what the store owner declared to be a slow spot in the evening crowd. He'd never dreamed the shop would've been so busy. He'd seen people coming in on dates, people heading to the bar that wanted a last

18

minute sugar buzz before they started drinking and folks stopping by after dinner for dessert. They all loved the ice cream. Although a few of the more health conscious had ordered sorbet or smoothies, most of the patrons indulged in the ice cream. Taking a long lick of the French Coconut Surprise cone he snagged for his own dinner, he wasn't surprised. *It's delicious. Easily the best ice cream I've ever had.*

Since he didn't have a name tag yet, several of the customers called him Dorothy. One even asked where Toto or the Lion was. *I'll get used to it eventually.* He had several friends that were overly catty and he'd noticed Bea Mann was being catty right back to some of the customers. *I can learn to do that. I just don't want to piss anyone off the first night on the job.*

On his way off the floor, Bea suggested he touch up his face a bit. Conrad looked in the mirror. *I can't tell what needs touching up.* Everything Bea applied earlier looked like it was fine. He'd never worn makeup before, and he didn't know anyone other than his mother and some of her friends who did. Licking his ice cream, Conrad tried to figure out what needed to be done.

"Cat, we need a hand!" Bea called sweetly in the distance.

Conrad barely registered the voice and kept licking his ice cream.

"Cat, some help would be appreciated!"

Wondering who Cat was, he continued working on his frozen milky dinner. Nobody else had come on duty since he'd been there.

"Conrad!" Dracanna's voice roared into the back room.

He jumped. *Shit, I forgot the name I chose.* Conrad's

ice cream fell out of his cone and on to the dressing room floor. Ignoring the spill, he raced for the front of the store.

"Sorry, I forgot my name," he stammered. The door to the backroom opened and Dracanna's angry, pinched face glared at him.

Her narrow shoulders heaved with a heavy sigh. "Just see that you figure out who you are, and quickly. As long as you're in this shop, you answer to Cat! Now, we're getting busy again out there, and we could really use a hand," Dracanna snarled. She turned her heels and stomped out to the sales floor.

Somewhere in the back room, Conrad thought he heard a light chuckle.

***

A chill struck Conrad. It felt like a wintery blast from an open door, but it was summer in Dallas. *Cold blasts don't happen in Dallas, especially this time of year.* He glanced toward the door while he handed his most recent customer their change. The man smiled and dropped a five in the tip jar. Conrad managed to say thanks before dropping his jaw at the seven-foot tall…thing that walked into Scary Queen. He couldn't see any clothes on it, but the long brown hair covered everything, except the face which reminded him more of a gorilla than a man.

What the hell is it? He turned to Bea, "Ah Bea, do you see what I see?"

The redhead looked up, then smiled. "Oh that's Sassy, don't mind him, he comes in now and again. Doesn't talk much, but I know what he wants."

"That *thing* comes in here regularly?" Conrad stammered, torn between running for his cell phone to get a picture and just plain running. Even his military training hadn't prepared him for seeing the tallest and hairiest *man?*

20

he'd ever seen. It looked like it belonged in a forest somewhere.

Bea reached over and patted Conrad on the arm. "Honey, you'll see all kinds of things working in here. You'd best get used to it. At least Sassy is friendly." She turned toward the approaching customer. "Heeeeyyyy Sassy, come in for your Rocky Road?"

The huge creature smiled. At least Conrad hoped it was a smile and not the thing bearing its teeth at his coworker. It pointed into the case and grunted.

"One scoop or two?" Bea asked, grabbing a waffle cone off the top of the Plexiglas counter.

It held up three long hairy fingers.

"Three scoops?" Bea laughed as she opened the counter door and reached in for the Rocky Road. "Aren't you the big spender tonight?"

The thing's heavy hands reached up and pushed back a lock of long brown hair out of its bulging face.

"Oh, you have a date? Why didn't you bring her here?" Bea settled the second scoop of the ice cream into the cone.

Sassy turned away and hid his face behind his hair.

"She's shy." Bea reached back into the case. "Well, you'll have to bring her around sometime. I'd love to meet her."

As Bea closed the case, the creature pointed a hairy finger to something nearer the register.

"You want sprinkles tonight?"

Its shaggy head nodded. Then its hands rose up in the air.

Bea waggled her finger at the creature. "Oh, I know you didn't just ask for extra sprinkles."

A deep huffing laugh came from Sassy's huge mouth.

With practiced ease, Bea lifted out two scoops of chocolate sprinkles and dumped them over the top of the ice cream. "Is that enough?"

Sassy nodded and held out his hand for the ice cream cone. Bea passed him the treat. Sassy smiled. He took almost half of the top scoop in one smooth lick. He gave Bea a thumbs up and turned for the door.

Conrad finally jolted out of his stare. "Hey, he didn't pay for that."

"Yeah he did," Bea replied. "He's got an account with Dracanna. Sometimes he brings in rare herbs that he finds and trades them for ice cream. Some of our more unusual guests have tabs like that. Here, let me show you." They went over to the cash register. Sitting wedged in between the side of the cash register and the counter was a tall, thin ledger. Bea opened the book and flipped till she found a page where "Sassy" was written in neat elegant script across the top. Bea's rough press-on nails trailed down the column.

"Yup, looks like ole` Sassy has about two hundred dollars on his account right now," Bea replied picking up a small red pen from the register's lip. She made a notation on the bottom of the list and subtracted out the cost of a triple scoop waffle cone. "He's good for a few more trips. Besides, where would he keep a wallet?"

Conrad stopped and thought about it. *Shit! I just saw a naked bigfoot, up close and personal and he's a regular here. I bet that means he'll be back in. What do I do if Bea isn't here to deal with him?* He reached for the counter to steady himself. "I thought they were supposed to be smelly."

Bea looked thoughtful for a moment. "Not sure about the rest of them, but Sassy never is. Always smells like a nice, clean pine-fresh forest. Hey, I noticed that the Quick Kiwi is out in the case, can you go pull another tub from the freezer? I need to run into the back for a moment while we're slow."

"Sure," Conrad said moving around the counter toward the freezer.

He opened the door, but couldn't find any Quick Kiwi. It had been there earlier when Bea showed him the back stock. They'd run out once already—about the time he took his lunch. *That must have been the last tub.* Conrad went back around to the case and looked in. Sure enough, there was barely a crust of light green ice cream in the bottom of the tub. Bea told him earlier to throw away empty tubs. He lifted the tub and carried it over to the trash bin, near the door to the back room.

Back at the case, Conrad looked down at the ice cream. All the rows had three tubs, except for the two on the far ends of the case. They had just two. The short ones, had the tubs pulled toward the back of the case, making it easier to serve. Conrad reached in and pulled the Rainbow Licorice closer to the Pinky Pie. As he did, a small jolt of electricity ran up his arm.

Before he had a chance to look around for the source of the shock, the shop bell clanked. A small Asian drag queen rushed in. She ran right up to the counter, her short school-girl skirt swirling around her gyrating hips.

She looked Conrad up and down with a critical eye. "You must be new. Where's Dracanna? I do hope you didn't drop a house on her or her sister."

Conrad couldn't help but stare. "He…she's in the back." *I've never been around drag queens on a regular basis. I've got to get it sorted out in my head. If they're wearing a dress, they're female, if not, they're male. I hope I don't get fired for my learning curve on that.*

She waved a petite oriental finger at him. "Oh child,

don't let her hear you call her a him. It will be the last thing you ever do here." Then she disappeared into the backroom.

The bell clanged again, and two men walked in. Conrad recognized one of them, the taller and cuter of the two, dressed in a blue and gold fancy western shirt, tan cowboy hat, and skin-tight blue jeans. He frequented the country bar down the block. He'd admired the man with his perfect chin, blond hair and blue eyes, for a long time. But he could never work up the nerve to go over and introduce himself. Glancing down at the blue gingham dress, his heart sank. Now Conrad was finally going to talk to the hunky guy, and he was in a blue dress and a wig. *I wonder if I could go in the back and have someone else come out and wait on them.*

"Look, why do we have to come in here?" the short plump man complained. He glared at the hunky blond cowboy. "You know I'm on a diet. You've been acting strange all night."

"I've been acting strange?" The cute guy turned on the other man. "You're the one who's been carrying on all night. We were supposed to have a nice night out on the town, but all you've been able to do is whine. I want some ice cream and then I want to go home."

"I bet you're going to eat that in front of me just to be mean!" the other guy screamed. "Fine, if you're going to be like that I'm going home. Alone! To my place! Without you!"

The blond rolled his eyes, lifted his cowboy hat and ran a large hand though his short hair.

"I'm really going to leave." The shorter man headed for the door. "I don't have to watch you fill yourself with all those calories."

Conrad wanted more than anything to crawl into the

backroom and have someone else come out and help. *This is so embarrassing. I never understand why couples fight in public. The way the hunky guy is acting, I doubt they've been dating long. The other guy seems kinda cold.*

The man opened the door and stood there while the warm wind from the street blew through and the noise from Cedar Springs poured in. It made Conrad realize that when the bigfoot came and went there had been more off than just the temperature. He didn't hear any street noises.

"Seriously, I'm going to leave you here!" the short guy called from the door. "You'll have to walk home!"

The blond's leather cowboy boots didn't move, and his handsome face remained impassive until the door close. "Is he gone?"

Conrad nodded. "Yeah, he's standing outside the door right now." The little man moved on down the sidewalk. "Okay, he's going away."

The cowboy's massive shoulders heaved as he let out a relieved sigh. "Thank, God. Our first date was nice enough, but he's been a little drama queen all night long. First he didn't want steaks, said he couldn't do red meat, and then he didn't want chicken. He finally said he'd eat fish, and what did he do? Announce he'd left his wallet at home. So, I got stuck with the whole check. Then he gives me grief about coming in here. I'm sorry, but after fish, I need some ice cream."

"So, what can I get you?" Conrad flashed him a big understanding smile.

The cowboy scanned through the case. "Are you new here? I don't recognize you."

"Yeah, just started today."

"Well, from what I can tell, you're a dang sight prettier than some of the gals they've had in here." He

25

offered his large hand across the counter to Conrad. "Name's Travis."

Conrad's heart shot up into his throat. The man he'd been lusting over, Travis, wanted to shake his hand. He reached for the offered hand and hoped that his wasn't too sweaty, or sticky, or anything else the man might find objectionable. "Conrad...I mean Cat Astrophe."

Travis's hand engulfed Conrad's.

He gulped.

The cowboy chuckled. "You don't look like a catastrophe, Conrad." He smiled with a flirty glint in his eyes.

Conrad tried to pull himself together. *Act cool. Be cool. Ice cream is cool.* "So, what can I get for you, Travis?"

Pressing nice, full lips together, Travis appeared to study the ice cream. "You know, so far, everything I've had here was completely awesome. I want to try something new. Give me two scoops of Rainbow Licorice in a chocolate waffle cone."

"Two scoops Rainbow Licorice in a chocolate waffle cone?" Conrad repeated.

Travis nodded. "That'd be it."

Conrad looked for a clean scoop and didn't see one. "Be right back, need to get a clean scoop." He hurried through the back door.

"I tell you, something's about to happen," a voice that Conrad didn't recognize was saying.

Dracanna and the Asian queen both looked up as he rushed in.

"Do you need something?" his boss asked. "We heard someone out front having a meltdown."

"Nope, we're just out of clean scoops." Conrad scanned the counter for an unsoiled scoop. He spotted one

26

that looked different, than the others sitting on the counter, more like an antique. Snatching it up, he ran back toward Travis.

"Cat, wait!" Dracanna shouted after him as the door closed.

Travis still stood waiting on the other side of the counter. Opening the ice-cream case, Conrad smiled at him.

"Sorry about that." He tried not to stammer. "We've had a busy night." He realized how silly that sounded since Travis was now the only customer in the shop and wished he hadn't said it.

"You guys are always hopping." The cowboy grinned at him, flashing a set of perfect teeth. "This is the first time I've ever come in that you didn't have someone in here. Normally there's a line, especially on the weekend."

Conrad loaded the first scoop into the cone. "It was really busy earlier, that's why we're out of clean scoops. The boss is in the back washing them now."

The door to the backroom flew open. Conrad turned. Dracanna stood there, a scowl lining her face and pink-gloved hands on her black-lace hips.

He had the second ball of ice cream in the scoop, and something about the dark expression on his boss's face caused him to jump. The extra-large serving of Rainbow Licorice fell into the half-full tub of Pinky Pie.

The strange voice he'd heard earlier screamed from Conrad's hand. "No!"

A bright flash of energy exploded out of the tub of Pinky Pie. Conrad flew into the wall behind him. Stars filled his eyes. When his vision cleared, a huge pink and rainbow ooze covered the ice cream counter, threatening Travis with long creamy tentacles. Dracanna slumped against the doorframe leading into the backroom. *I've got to do something*. Looking across the counter, he spotted the butcher knives they used to cut up fresh fruit for smoothies. *They're dirty, but they'll have to do.* His military training kicked in. He grabbed up four and threw himself over the counter. *I've got to save Travis.*

"Travis, catch!" He gestured with the knives.

The cowboy picked up one of the tables and smashed it down into the ice cream creature. The table sank into the monster like a hot spoon in room-temperature ice cream.

The whole shop shook like there'd been an earthquake, but they were in Dallas. *Dallas didn't have earthquakes.* Conrad's heart raced. *What is this thing? It looks and smells like an animated pile of pink ice cream. Ice cream doesn't try to eat people. It normally works the other way around.*

"Conrad, throw it!" Travis called out.

Conrad tossed a knife to Travis, careful to make a throw he could easily catch. The cowboy caught the knife and held up the other hand for a second one. Conrad made that toss too and then he waded in on the ice cream monster.

Slashing with the knife, Conrad managed to cut off big soupy globes of it, but the thing still advanced on Travis. Travis cut gallantly at the thing. Then one of his knives imbedded in the creature.

"Travis, look out!" Conrad shouted as a tentacle of ice cream shot out of the thing to strike the man in the side of his perfect face. The sweet, dripping appendage pulled the cowboy toward the body of the beast. Conrad tried to make it around to the other side of the corrupted confectionary, but he slipped in the monster's melting runoff.

Conrad caught himself on one of the round tables. He grabbed it by the top and swung the metal legs at the tentacle that clutched at Travis. The table's legs sliced through the tentacle and slammed into the tile floor. The impact snapped the legs off, but with the tentacle severed, Travis collapsed to the floor.

"Not the tables!" Dracanna screamed. She'd moved from the door and stood pale, clinging to the cash register.

Bea and the Asian queen crowded through the doorway. "What in the Hell?!?" Bea exclaimed.

"Where's Scoop?" Dracanna shouted as Conrad swung the busted table back into the body of the monster.

Conrad ran for Travis. The cowboy wasn't moving. He grabbed hold of the Travis's broad shoulders and pulled him toward the far corner of the room. *I hope the monster won't have time to get here before it melts.* Travis moaned as Conrad laid the man as gently as possible on the cold tile floor. Grabbing a chair, he held it like a lion tamer between them and the advancing glob of putrid pink ice cream. *I wish I had more than a chair and a knife.*

Ignoring the commotion behind the counter, Conrad kept his eyes on the monster, which wasn't melting nearly as fast as he wished it would. A tentacle shot out from it and Conrad used the chair to bat it away. Another tentacle connected with the side of his head. Conrad slipped on the floor as the monster pulled him toward the now pulsating pink pile.

"Where the hell is Scoop?!" Dracanna screeched.

Who is Scoop? Conrad tried to maintain his footing on the slick floor. He didn't want to get consumed by the ice cream creature.

A distant voice, the one Conrad didn't recognize, shouted. "I'm over here, you blind bitch, on top of the freezer!"

The monster pulled him closer. He struggled. Unfortunately the last knife didn't make a dent in the

29

tentacle. On the second slash, the blade hit something and stuck. Conrad hoped it was only ice. The thing smashed through another table. The shop lurched again. This time tables and chairs fell. The cash register toppled with a huge crash.

Bea's strong hands closed around Conrad's legs. "Hang on sweetie. We're trying to get you out of this."

"What *is* this *thing*?" Conrad reached up and grabbed the tentacle that slid across the side of his face. His fingers sank into the ice cream, but he couldn't find anything to hold on to.

"Looks like Pinky Pie with a dash of Rainbow Licorice," Bea said as she tried to pull Conrad away from the thing. "Other than that, it's a bit weird, even for this place." Her artificial nails dug into his leg as the drag queen fought for a better hold.

The blob's tentacle was close enough to the pulsating mass that all Conrad could see was the undulating pink mass of ice cream. He tried to scream as it pulled his head into the sweat sticky mass, but the ice cream covered his mouth before he could open it. *Mom's going to be pissed if I ruin her blue dress.*

Ice cream engulfed Conrad. *How long will I survive before I suffocate in the sticky depths of dairy?* He shook with cold and gagged at the overwhelming stench of rotting strawberries. It pulled him deeper and at last Bea let go of his leg as the monster fully engulfed him.

A light feeling soothed him as he floated in the gooey mess. *Am I about to lose consciousness, or have I already died and is this the way people feel before they go to Heaven?*

2
Apple Avalanche

Sensation returned to Conrad Bane's limbs. The ice cream monster lay as a pile of melted pink slop. *I can breathe!* Conrad lay there for several minutes taking long gasping breaths, trying to get air back into his system.

"I think you're going to be okay, honey," Bea said at his side.

"What happened? How did I get out of that?" he heaved.

"Oh, Dracanna got the energies of the control console in the ice-cream counter realigned and dispelled the demon. It wasn't too hard, once Scoop explained what she needed to do."

With his head pounding, Conrad couldn't follow anything she said, so he hoped his next question would have a more comprehensible answer. "How's Travis?"

"Who's Travis?" Bea asked. "Oh, that cute cowboy over here? He's sitting up. I think he'll be fine. Well, at least until Dracanna gets a hold of him, and *you* for breaking tables."

"Why, what do tables have to do with anything?" Conrad's mind was fuzzy. *All I want to do is go home and never see the Scary Queen Ice-Cream Shop again.*

***

Dracanna stared at the wreckage of the shop and shook her head. "Is this what you were afraid of?" She glared at Scoop.

"I felt something wrong," Scoop replied.

"Wrong doesn't begin to describe the mess we're in now!" Dracanna slammed the metal implement on the counter with more force than she intended. *We have to get things back in order and quickly. There was no telling what type of damage we've done with our unintended departure.*

"Rice! Bea! Cat! Get the tables upright and let's assess the damage here," she called out to her crew.

"What happened?" Cat scraped ice cream off her dress.

"Do you want the long story or the short one?" Dracanna snapped.

"Kid it's like this," Scoop started, still lying on the counter, "You accidently created a magical blending of ice cream in the counter. The Rainbow Pinky Pie Licorice beast then ransacked the shop, destroying its moorings, and casting us off in time and space."

Cat looked confused. "Who's talking and what is he…she…it talking about?"

"We normally call it a 'he', but 'it' works too." Dracanna smiled. "Gals, set up a few tables and let's explain all this to Cat Astrophe and," she looked over at the cowboy sitting on the floor near the wall, "the cowboy over there." She picked up Scoop and headed into the destroyed dining area. Carefully avoiding the growing puddle of melting pink ice cream, she moved to where Rice had a table set up

32

correctly and accepted the chair Bea offered. Cat helped the cowboy to his feet.

Once everyone had a chair, she set Scoop down on the table and took a deep dramatic breath. "Now then, Cat and Cowboy, you may not have been aware of it before, but this ice cream shop is actually the nexus of a rip in time and space. Our control system is the ice cream counter. We're always very careful about the configuration of the tubs of ice cream in there. Each tub—or maybe the better term here is each flavor—has its special spot. When we run out of a particular flavor, we always replace it with another tub of the same flavor. That keeps the energy of the control system running correctly. There's a special place for each limited edition flavor that has nothing to do with the rest of the system."

"So are you saying when I moved the Rainbow Licorice next to the Pinky Pie, I caused all the problems?" Cat pulled off the ruined brown bob wig and shook some of the ice cream out of it. The pink droplets splattered onto the white tile.

"You started the problem," Dracanna said. "If we'd had more of a warning, we could've stopped it from escalating. The kiwis in the Quick Kiwi help balance the conflicting energies of the strawberries in the Pinky Pie with the wild licorice in the Rainbow Licorice. When you dropped the scoop of Rainbow Licorice into the tub of Pinky Pie the radical change in energies called forth an extra-dimensional ice-cream demon."

"A what?" The cowboy's southern drawl a little thicker than Dracanna expected. "This is nuts. There are no such things as extra-dimensional ice-cream demons. The 'cute and interesting' in this shop just left the building. I'm out of here." He headed for the door.

"Honey, I wouldn't do that if I were you," Bea warned as he stomped toward the exit.

As he opened the door, a frigid blast of air screamed through the shop. After a moment things seemed to equalize, but for a second, it felt like they were all about to be sucked outside. The cowboy stopped, looking out into the vast darkness that now greeted him where a street had been a short time earlier. "What in the hell?"

Bea walked up behind him, gently pulled him back into the shop by his belt and closed the door. "Look, Travis, why don't you go over and finish hearing what Dracanna has to say." She patted his arm and led him back to the table.

"What in the hell was outside that door," Cat demanded. "Where the hell are we?"

Dracanna took another deep breath. "As to what is outside the door, well… that's deep space. As to where the hell we are, we won't know *that* until we get the ice cream counter cleaned and sorted out. Right now, we are hurtling through time and space with no sure way of knowing where or when we are. For all I know, we're on a collision course with disaster and we're wreaking havoc on the very fabric of reality."

"How do we stop it?" Cat asked.

"First thing we have to do is get all the tables and chairs set up right again," the store owner replied.

Cat put her hands on her blue gingham hips with a squishing noise. "What does that have to do with anything?"

"The positions of the chairs on the grid of the floor helps moor the ship to a spot in time and space," Dracanna explained. "If the tables are moved around, that changes *where* we go. If the chairs are moved around in a certain order, that affects *when* we go."

"That's stupid," Travis said, still looking disturbed

34

from his view out the door. "People move the tables and chairs around all the time."

Dracanna stared at the pretty cowboy. "Sweetie, I've seen you in here before. Have you ever seen anyone do more than pull a chair out to sit in it? Have you ever seen a table out of place?"

A thoughtful look crossed the ruggedly handsome face. "Can't say as I have. But how do you clean the place?"

"Very carefully," Rice Pilaf replied. "And this mess is going to take a lot of cleaning tonight." She glared at Cat. "I think you really are a Catastrophe."

Ignoring her, Dracanna continued, "Each table and chair has a certain distance that they can be moved within the confines of the shop. Look there." She pointed to colored lines on the floor that looked like grout lines in the tables. Each set of colored lines formed an intricate geometric pattern and each pattern was a different color. Then she gestured to the tables, which had grout lines that matched the color of the lines in the floor. "As long as the table with the strawberry lines is within the strawberry area on the floor, everything's fine. But move it over to the lime area, and we have a problem. That shaking we felt earlier was the shop becoming unmoored. When you two," she shook a blue-nailed finger at Cat and Travis, "used the tables to fight off the ice cream demon, you disrupted the grid. Now that you broke some tables, we're going to have to replace them before we can get back to where we belong."

"You realize, they broke the blueberry table and the raspberry crème one?" Scoop asked.

"And what is that?" Cat pointed at the antique implement lying on the table.

"On the outside, he's a lowly ice cream scoop. On the inside, he's a spirit trapped inside a lowly ice cream scoop."

Dracanna said. The weight of the situation fell heavily on her skinny shoulders. *The next time someone tries to use the name Cat Astrophe they'll be fired before they had a chance to cause one. Now I can only hope that we have the needed tables, if not, I might not be able to get us home in one piece. We'll be trapped tumbling through space and time until the ice cream runs out and we starve to death. Even though I'll be the last to go, it's about to get cold and lonely in this little inter-dimensional ice cream shop. Scoop and I will be trapped together forever, long after the others are gone.*

***

Conrad stood in the cluttered storeroom surveying the astounding assortment of restaurant paraphernalia packed into the apparently unlimited space. He and Travis found a great pile of café tables right next to the chairs. Some of the seats were of strange designs. Things he'd never seen before. They bent and curved in directions that would have been most uncomfortable for him to sit in. But most had the same basic colored grout patterning on them, indicating they went with the various tables.

"What color did she say we were looking for?" Travis lifted another table from the stack.

"Blueberry," Conrad replied.

"What the hell color is 'blueberry'?"

"Do I look that gay?"

"You were the one in the dress," Travis replied.

Conrad put his hand on his hips, happy to feel jeans there again. "Yeah, that was my work uniform. I've never worn a dress before this afternoon." Conrad was relieved when Dracanna pronounced the blue gingham dress a total loss after the defeat of the ice cream demon, even though it would mean a lengthy explanation to his mother. Luckily they'd found a pair of jeans and a tank top in the dressing room. The jeans were several sizes too big, but Bea fashioned a belt out of a red silk scarf. The look was either a little too piratey or a little too prissy. He couldn't decide which.

Travis put down the table he held and smiled at Conrad. "Well, I think you look a lot better this way, without the dress and makeup."

Heat rose in Conrad's face. "Thanks." *He likes the way I look.*

"Yup, definitely cuter without the makeup." Travis chuckled and went back to digging through the tables. Several minutes later, he raised a table above his head. "You think this is 'blueberry'?" He pointed the table top toward Conrad.

Staring at the grout around the black tiles, he shrugged. "Maybe. It might also be a royal blue. Why don't we go and see what Dracanna says about it." Conrad reached to take the table from Travis so he'd be able to wade out of the mass of wrong-colored tables. They navigated back through several storage rooms before they finally reemerged in the backroom of Scary Queen.

Rice Pilaf stood at the big mixing vat, pouring cream. "Why didn't I just stay home? It was my night off and I had a feeling to come in, just in time to have the store go blasting off. I should've stayed home and watched the Joan Collins marathon on Lifetime." There wasn't anyone else around.

Conrad hoped they could make it past the oriental queen without being noticed. She'd been going on like this for a couple of hours. She seemed to focus her anger at him whenever their paths crossed. In the seemingly-small shop, it was more often than he liked. Behind him, Travis closed the door a little too loud and Rice's gaze snapped in his direction.

"Oh, and here she is now! *Cat Astrophe*," Rice sniped. "How's it feel, dearie, to do more damage on your first day than some of us who have been here for years?"

Conrad squared his shoulders. It wasn't his fault Bea and Dracanna hadn't explained anything important to the more complex workings of the shop, or spaceship, he couldn't exactly decide the correct word. "I'm sorry, I thought I was working in an ice cream shop, not some strange spaceship."

Rice wrinkled her nose. "It's easy to make excuses. But I know how the girls are, and Dracanna was in a state today. I guess I can forgive you this once. But," she pointed a bright red nail at Conrad, "screw up one more time, and I'll show you the little-known martial art of Karageshia."

Shaking his head and not wanting to argue with his coworker, Conrad resumed walking. "I'll try to do better."

"Bit of a bitch, isn't she?" Travis leaned in and whispered.

Conrad held the door open so he could get the table through. "I'm not sure having a job is worth this," he replied quietly.

The dining room was regaining a semblance of order. Bea had finally gotten all the sticky remains of the ice-cream demon up. The tile floor sparkled with her efforts. All but the broken tables were returned to their correct positioning. A couple of chairs were also missing.

"Okay, let's see that table," Bea said. As they walked toward her, she leaned on the handle of the well-used mop in her rubber-gloved hands. Travis showed her the table top. She nodded.

"That's the one." She pointed to the spot on the floor where it belonged. "Now we need to find the raspberry crème one, and this shop should be able to anchor somewhere."

Travis looked perplexed. His broad forehead wrinkled in thought. "What color is 'raspberry crème'?"

Bea raised a bushy eyebrow at him. "Honey, come on over here." She grabbed their elbows and led them over to the spot on the floor that had a couple of chairs but no table. She pointed down. "See that color?"

They both nodded.

"That's 'raspberry crème'. It's not 'soft rose', or 'blushing plum'. It's 'raspberry crème'. There should be a couple of tables in the back with that color grout."

Something roared behind the counter. As they turned, a stream of purple ice cream plumed up, striking the ceiling. The shop shuddered.

Conrad grew lightheaded. *Oh, please, God, I don't think I can fight another ice cream demon right now. Okay, ever. I really just want to go home and never ever go to a drag show, ever again. I'm not even sure I'll be able to eat ice cream without flashing back to that pink monstrosity that tried to eat me.*

"Gods damn it!" Dracanna shouted as purple ice cream gushed down on her.

"Why don't you two go find that table? The sooner we stabilize, the sooner she can get things back in order over there." Bea made shooing motions with her pink glove-covered hands as she dashed toward the counter, snatching up a dish towel.

Conrad sighed. *This adventure can't end soon enough. I want to be back home in Dallas, Texas, not off in deep space tumbling through time if Dracanna's telling the truth.* He glanced at the strange little woman as they walked into the backroom. Dracanna yanked the dish towel out of

Bea's hand with a growl. She wiped purple ice cream off her face with a disgusted look.

"Have you seen any 'raspberry crème' tables back there?" Travis asked as the door swung shut.

Conrad shook his head. "Not a one. I guess we'll just have to dig."

"We *have* been digging. This has got to be one of the most ludicrous situations I've ever been in."

"So, have you been thrown through time and space before?" Conrad looked around for Rice Pilaf, but she was nowhere to be seen. The mixing vat was deserted, but water still ran in the sink.

Travis chuckled. It was a deep, pleasant sound. "No, actually the most ludicrous situation I've been in before this was getting a flat tire while on the way to a costume party with this really flamboyant guy I was dating at the time. He had no idea of how to change a tire and was afraid of breaking a nail, and I was dressed as a space man in silver lame. Needless to say, that was a night I wanted to forget. Getting mud and grease all over my costume was bad, but listening to him have a hysterical meltdown was worse."

Conrad smiled as he opened the door into the storeroom. "See, you've played dress up before."

Travis smiled back. "But, *I* didn't look like Dorothy."

The shop suddenly tilted, throwing Conrad into Travis, and the two of them into the wall. Tables, chairs, and many things he couldn't identify, crashed down around them. Several of the tables shattered, sending colored shards of tile and grout flying in all directions. Somehow, nothing hit them, although a pile of tablecloths landed right next to Conrad's head. Pressed under him, Travis' body felt hard and lean.

"Now what?" Travis asked. The orientation of the

shop remained at the odd angle with the wall where the ceiling should be, like some bizarre Escher painting.

"No clue, let's find that table and get out front and see if we can lend a hand." Conrad struggled to stand up on the wall.

"And how are we going to find a 'raspberry crème' table now?" Travis got to his feet.

Conrad glanced back at the chaotic mess in the topsy-turvy storeroom. "Not sure we could find it now but let's move this stuff around and see what we can find," he muttered. "The way our luck has been going, it's one of the ones that smashed."

They searched until Conrad came up with a handful of raspberry crème' powder. He held his hand out toward Travis. "What do you want to bet, this came from the only raspberry crème' table left back here and now it's been smashed to bits?"

Travis nodded after studying Conrad's hand for a moment. "I bet you're right." He frowned. "So what do we do now?"

"Now we go break the news to Dracanna and hope that she has some way to get us back to Dallas." Conrad dropped the pile of reddish purple dust on the floor and brushed off his hands. He reached down for the doorknob that was now on the floor, then held the door open so that Travis could hunch over and slide through. The sound of water running came through the open door. Travis stumbled and caught hold of the door frame.

"Hold on, Conrad," he said. "We've got a bit of a problem."

"What now?"

"The floor...ah, wall is several feet down. Looks like the whole shop turned on its side."

"That kinda makes sense, seeing as we're standing on the wall here. I guess it's a good thing it didn't tip the other way. That might've been a painful fall."

"Okay, I can jump down from this doorway, but how do we get back up to the other door?" Travis asked.

"We could take some of these tablecloths and make a rope." Conrad reached down and picked up a bright green cloth. There were enough colors that they'd be able to make a fairly long and festive colored rope. *Might work really great for a gay pride float decoration. I hope I get to go to another pride someday.*

"Sounds good, toss them to me once I get through the door." Travis turned and crouched down to get through the door and jumped. He splashed down. "Shit, there's water all over the place down here."

"Probably from the sink Rice Pilaf was using." Conrad handed the first of the tablecloths through to Travis.

The mess in the backroom was worse than in the storage room. Dissolving sugar and other ingredients lay in a huge puddle of water which cascaded down from the sink that now hung on the wall about twenty feet above them. The water was still running, causing a bit of a waterfall effect.

"We need to get that water turned off," said Conrad, stepping out of the fall of soapy wetness.

"How are we going to do that?" Travis asked "That's too far up there for either of us to reach."

Conrad looked up at the industrial metal sink. Heavy steel legs supported the basin that appeared to be bolted to the wall. The water poured out of the faucet and made the long drop toward the floor.

"The tablecloths," he said. "Maybe the rope idea will work here too. If we can get a rope up there, one of us can climb up and turn off the water."

"So Conrad, if the shop has left Dallas and is traveling through space, how do we still have water running?"

Conrad shook his head. "Not sure, even more reason to get the water turned off. We don't need to run out of water before we get this thing landed."

Travis began tying tablecloths together. "We don't know how well anchored the thing is. You're a bit smaller than I am. Think you can make it up there?" He smiled.

Conrad glanced up at the sink and sighed. He'd never been that good at climbing the rope in basic training, but he'd never had a hunky guy like Travis holding his rope before either. He swallowed and reached for another tablecloth to help Travis.

"We'll see," he mumbled.

Once the makeshift rope was finished, Travis managed to toss it over the counter leg. He worked the tablecloths until he had hold of both ends. He braced himself as Conrad grabbed hold.

"I'll try and keep it as still as possible. " Travis smiled.

Conrad gulped. "Thanks."

Halfway up the impromptu rope, Conrad's arm started burning. *More time at the gym working on upper body.* By the time his hands closed around the metal sink leg fifteen feet above Travis, his arms ached, and his hands shook. He hefted himself up to the sink's edge. His fingers slipped on the slick, wet metal. He fell backward. His legs, twined in the tablecloths, stopped his fall, but his back screamed in pain.

"Shit!" Travis shouted below him. "Conrad, are you okay?"

Gasping for a breath, Conrad reached for the cloth

rope and righted himself, trying to ignore the pain in his back as he regained his grip on the sink's leg. "I will be."

He clung to the bottom of the sink for several minutes, willing his heart to slow down and his breathing to balance out before he tried again to get to the running faucet.

Swallowing hard, he forced himself to reach up again. This time he was ready for the slick metal surface and felt higher on the side of the sink for a drier spot. Keeping the tablecloths tight in his legs, he managed to pull himself high enough to turn off the faucet. As the water stopped, he realized he had been lucky and the angle of his climb had been out of the flow. It would've been much harder to climb up if the water had been hitting him the whole way.

"Well, that was the hard part," Travis called up. "Now, can you just slide down?"

Conrad didn't reply. With shaky hands, he moved his grip back to the cloth rope and started down.

"You know," Travis said. "If you still had on the dress, I might have an interesting view."

"It was a dress, not a kilt!" Conrad's hands screamed as he gripped the fabric again. His back complained as his whole body tensed.

Below him, Travis laughed. "And I bet you're not Scottish."

About halfway down his hands hit a worn spot on the rope. It jerked, giving a short rip and sending him scrambling. "Shit!" Conrad shouted as he tried to get a better grip. He tried to wrap his feet in the cloth, but his socks were wet and even with Travis holding it below him, it swung more than he could handle. He fell. He and Travis crashed into the wet wall beneath them.

"I tried to catch you," Travis said with a silly grin.

Conrad sighed. "Thanks. Are you all right?" *Wow, I'm*

a royal klutz. At least he tried to catch me and gave me another opportunity to touch him. He does have a nice body.

Travis laughed weakly. "As all right as I think I'm going to be until we get out of this mess."

Conrad pushed himself up, trying not to let his hands linger too long on Travis's broad chest. "I hear you."

"Now we're both wet." Travis sat. "I doubt they have more men's clothes around here."

"You never know, but the dressing room is behind…under that door." Conrad pointed at the door in the floor. A couple of feet from where they stood, it was barely outlined in the sugar, cream and assorted fruit and nut toppings. The heavy smell of strawberries mixed with a whiff of smashed peaches giving the area a unique aroma. "If it's oriented like the rest of the rooms we've been in so far, the door's in the ceiling."

"Should we check to see if anyone's down there?"

"Let's get out front. If we're missing someone, we can come back," Conrad replied.

They walked over the door and across the wall to the next wall.

"The door is on the other side of the desk," said Travis, looking up at the desk that appeared glued to the wall above them. Unlike the sink, the desk didn't have any exposed legs they could get the makeshift rope around. "And it opens toward the desk; that'll be tricky."

"We need to get over the desk first," said Conrad. "Do you think you could support my weight if I climb up on your shoulders?"

Travis smiled. "I can dead lift my own weight." He gave Conrad an appraising look. "I can probably support you. This wasn't how I imagined you crawling over me for the first time."

Conrad started to reply and blinked. "You've imagined me crawling over you?"

Travis chuckled. "Dude, tonight wasn't the first time I ever saw you. Of course the dress and wig threw me off a bit. But, I remember seeing you at the bar from time to time."

"We'll come back to this later," said Conrad, a warm blush started on his face. *He was watching me at the bar while I was watching him. We've got to get out of this mess and see where this can lead.* "Why don't you use the wall for a little extra balance and I'll climb up your back."

"Okay." A goofy grin crossed Travis's rugged face.

The cowboy's strong shoulders felt good under Conrad's hands. He pushed the thoughts of what he'd like to do to the man out of his mind, trying to envision him as a big log he had to heft himself up on. He tried to get a foot on Travis's calf, but the man cried out.

"Watch the toes!"

"The toes? Oh crap. Sorry. I balance better on my toes" Conrad made himself perch flat footed, so he wasn't jabbing Travis.

"No problem." Travis chuckled.

Conrad put his hands back on Travis's broad shoulders. "Okay, let's try this again." He heaved and started up Travis's hard body. His socks slipped a bit on the tight, wet blue jeans, but without too much trouble and using the wall for a little extra balance, he managed to stand on Travis's shoulders. From there, he was able to reach up, get a hold on the desk and pull himself up until he stood on the far side near the door.

"Toss me the tablecloths, and I'll support you while you climb up," he called down to Travis as he shifted his body several times to make sure the desk was going to hold up to their weight.

It took two tries to get the makeshift rope up to Conrad.

"Not that good at roping, are ya cowboy?" Conrad called down with a chuckle. He wrapped the tablecloth rope around his waist.

Travis laughed back. "It's been a while."

Conrad braced himself the best he could against the wall and with his socks on the desk's slick side. "Okay, I think I'm ready." Without a word, Travis climbed the rope. Conrad slipped forward until he braced his feet on the lip where the top of the desk overlapped the side.

"Almost there!" Travis called as Conrad's back began to ache.

"Doing okay." He ignored the strain and didn't want to appear weak in front of the man he was growing more and more interested in. The impromptu rope around his waist tightened sharply and made his back scream in pain again.

When Travis had made it high enough that he could grab the desk and pull himself the rest of the way up, Conrad wanted to cry out in joy.

Then the shop shook again.

"Now what?" Conrad unwound the tablecloths from his waist, and pulled it up so it piled on the side of the desk at his feet. *We just got all the way up here, this better not be something that's going to throw us across the room. I don't know if I can get back to this door. I wonder if this is the time to complain about letting crazy drag queens fly a spaceship. And that's nothing I ever thought would go through my head.*

"Maybe they're about to get this thing straightened out." Travis got to his feet on the side of the desk next to him.

Conrad tried to breathe in the heavy musky smell of Travis' fresh sweat without too much noise. *No sense in enjoying this too much.* "We can hope." Conrad turned to reach for the door knob.

***

Dracanna frowned at the ice cream counter, now on the wall more than ten feet above her head. She hated it when the gravity went wonky. It made life very difficult when rooms were in the wrong orientation.

"What in the hell just happened?" Bea asked from the other side of the display freezers that blocker her from view.

"Minor problem with the gravity orientation array," Dracanna replied. "When I can get back up to the control panel, I should be able to fix it, if all the Apple Avalanche hasn't dumped out of the carton."

"Then you better get your high heels up here," Scoop's voice came from the cooler, "because it's threatening to run into the 'Caramel Custard Crème' and that won't be pretty."

"The new kid's not nearby, is he?" the store owner asked.

"Nope," Bea replied. "She and the cowboy just went into the back looking for the last table."

"Are the tables still in place?" The freezer blocked Dracanna's view of the dining room, but there hadn't been a major crash of tables and chairs. *I really don't want to know if the stabilization moorings are all out of place again. It's too much to hope for that everything stayed where they belonged, but with the way this day is going.*

"We dodged that bullet," Bea replied. "Everything is just fine out here. Well, as fine as anything can be that just went from being on the floor to on the wall. My mop water on the other hand, has gone all over the place, including me.

48

When you get this fixed, I need to get in the back and find a new ensemble. Including a new set of press-ons. I'll have you know I popped a nail hitting the wall…floor…whatever."

Dracanna glared in Bea's direction even though she couldn't see the drag queen. "Sure, might as well look our best for this catastrophe." She looked up at the case. It was still open from where she'd been working before the gravity shift. Taking a deep breath, and focusing on the metal counter leg above her, she jumped. Using an other-worldly agility that she tried to keep hidden, she managed to grab hold of the metal leg and hoist herself up to the open door of the ice cream case.

Scoop sat in between the rows of ice cream tubs, balanced precariously on the edge of a tub. Some of the 'Berry Surprise' dripped onto him.

"You better do something quick." Scoop sounded like he scowled, as if the possessed ice cream scoop even had the ability to scowl.

"Working on it." Dracanna leveraged herself up so she could get a hand on the disorganized ice cream tubs in the case. *I've got to remember to not wear tight dresses to work. A loose skirt would've made this a lot easier.* Starting with the Apple Avalanche, she worked her way down the case getting the tubs back in the correct order. It took a few minutes, and her wiry arms felt like they were made of lead from the effort of moving herself along the case, but when she reached the last one, Zebra Zippersnapps, the shop shuddered just as the door to the backroom opened.

***

As Conrad opened the door to the sales floor, the shop shuddered again. He clung to the doorframe as he spotted Dracanna hanging on to the serving counter. Gravity went back to normal. His grip on the doorframe gave out and once again, he and Travis ended up pressed together on the floor. This time Conrad was on the bottom. He groaned at the cowboy's sudden weight against him. His back screamed again. But he found the feeling of closeness ended too quickly as Travis stood, then offered him a hand up. Their hands stayed together just a little longer than need be, and Travis smiled at him warmly.

"I hope you found the 'raspberry crème' table," Dracanna snapped at Conrad, breaking the moment and Travis's smile.

"Sorry, we just got back there then everything shifted. We found a handful of raspberry crème' powder, so I thought we'd come see if you needed help up here," Conrad replied.

Dracanna's lips pulled back in a sneer, and her dark eyes radiated hate out like black laser beams. "What we need right now is that table so we can get moored somewhere and then I can get us back to Earth."

Before anyone could say anything else, the front door of the shop opened and a short man with a heavy fur coat and a conical felt hat trimmed in red fox fur walked in. A large curved sword hung at his side. Everyone stared as he walked toward the counter.

"Are you open for business?" he asked in slightly-accented English.

Conrad's mind reeled. *It's summer time in Dallas, why is this little man wearing such a fur coat? If they aren't on Earth anymore like Dracanna and Bea said, then how is he speaking English?* He glanced at his boss. She was whiter than normal, staring at the customer walking across the tile floor toward them.

"We are always open to humbly serve honored

customers." Dracanna bowed slightly to the man.

"Good," said the man. A slight smile crossed his lips, causing his thin dark mustache to lift in the corners. "Your arrival is an unexpected pleasure. I shall inform the Kahn, and we shall return." He turned and walked out before anyone could say a word.

3
Strawberry Stampede

As the door to Scary Queen swung shut, Dracanna snatched Scoop out of the ice cream display. Conrad stepped further into the room, wanting to see what was going on.

"Where in the hell are we?" Dracanna demanded shaking the utensil.

"I believe we're on Mongoleon," Scoop replied, "based on his dress and accent."

Dracanna reached under the counter and flipped a couple of switches. The counter shifted slightly and a huge holographic display popped up over the ice cream tubs. It reminded Conrad of the universal maps he'd seen in the planetarium. There was a series of stars with planets around them. It was in extreme 3D. Everything looked sharp enough to touch and have it feel solid. The vivid colors and movements took his breath away. *I didn't see that coming. That's a lot better tech than even the military has.*

"How is it we're not moving through time and space?" Dracanna asked.

"Something happened when the gravity righted itself,"

Scoop said. "We should be stable here until we can affect repairs."

Dracanna didn't reply. She just studied the map, running a talon-like hand through her ebony hair. The perfect nails on her other hand skimmed over the points on the map as Conrad and Travis stepped closer. A small red dot, off to the far right in a dense cluster of what Conrad took to be stars, blinked in a way that had to mean it was their current location.

Conrad pointed at the dot. "I presume that's us?"

"Of course it's us," Dracanna snarled. "There's no red pulsars in this part of space, so the red flashing light has to be us." She swept her hand over the display, and it changed. Now a single world, brown and desert-like swirled on the hologram. The little red light was now in the middle of what appeared to be the central continent.

Dracanna sighed. "Great, we're just outside the main village of Genghis on the continent of Kahn. I bet the old man himself will be here any minute. Just what we did *not* need today."

"Wait a minute," Conrad's brain tied itself in knots trying to absorb all the new information that was cascading over him. It was quickly getting to be too much. "We're about to meet Genghis Kahn? So, we really did travel back in time?"

"Not really, kid," his boss replied. "Scoop, explain it. I need to go find Rice. The Kahn prefers to be served by Asians. Bea, get that floor cleaned up before he arrives." Dracanna turned away from the counter and stormed into the backroom.

Conrad looked at the ice cream scoop, waiting for an explanation. *Am I really standing here on an alien planet waiting for a chunk of metal to tell me what's going on?* As more and more strange things happened, they started being easier to accept.

"Well, Conrad, Travis, it's like this," Scoop began. "It appears our movement through time was not as extreme as our movement through space. We are now on the outer rim of the Milky Way Galaxy, but not before you were born. In truth, it looks like we haven't traveled in time at all. We're sitting on the planet Mongoleon, which was conquered over two thousand years ago by Genghis Kahn and his Mongol army after they took over a small space craft that was visiting Earth on a scientific mission."

"Wait a minute, are you saying that aliens have been visiting Earth for centuries?" The opportunity to ask questions helped Conrad start sorting out what was happening.

"Don't knock it, Cat." Bea swung her mop around the floor in front of the counter. "Some of those aliens can give the most interesting anal probes. Trust me."

"Actually, longer than that," Scoop continued as if ignoring Bea. "The scientists, I was talking about, were members of a race that your common culture likes to refer to as the 'Grays'. They weren't strong enough to overpower the barbarian horde once it invaded the ship. It didn't take long for Genghis and his followers to learn everything the Grays could teach them. They spent time terrorizing the space lanes until Genghis grew tired and wanted to settle down. By then, one of his sons had assumed the title of Kahn back on Earth, so Genghis, being the awesome soul that he is, decided to expand his empire. He found a world that reminded him of the Mongolian desert and conquered it. Overall, a very tidy operation. They got rid of most of the intelligent life on the planet but still have a bit of a problem with some of the more elusive species. In the ensuing

54

millennia, using what was originally Gray technology, he has expanded his empire to encompass a large chunk of this arm of the Milky Way."

"But this is the *original* Genghis Kahn that's about to come into this shop?" Travis asked.

Scoop made an exasperated sound. "Of course it's the original. He used Gray tech to extend his lifespan. He's over two thousand years old, but doesn't look a day over forty-five."

"We've got riders approaching," Bea called from the front. She wheeled her mop bucket toward the backroom.

"Conrad, let Dracanna know," Scoop said. "Travis, make sure all the tables and chairs are in order then get back in the back. Your clothes are wet. We can't have that. There should be something you can change into in the dressing room."

"I ain't wearing a dress," Travis growled.

"You shouldn't have to," Scoop retorted. "Now get the chairs and tables in order, then get back there."

Conrad dashed for the back of the store. The backroom was in as big a mess as he expected. The puddle of water had sloshed from the wall back to the floor. Bea swished her mop around, cleaning it up. All along the wall, items that had been thrown to the floor when the shop first turned on its side were now piled in a mass of damp confusion.

"Did you see Dracanna?" Conrad asked his coworker.

"Nope, she wasn't in here when I wheeled back." Bea wrung out the wet mop. "I bet she's in the dressing room. No tracks through the sugar over there." She gestured with the mop handle at the area in front of the storage room door.

"Thanks." Conrad smiled and hurried toward the dressing room.

Dracanna stood in the midst of major chaos. It looked like every one of the many racks of clothes had been knocked over, scattering various shades of lame, velvet, and sequined attire everywhere. Here and there, wigs dotted the scene like hairy polka dots. The two dressing mirrors appeared intact, and the chairs were still upright, but all the makeup and accoutrements were scattered on the floor.

"I think Rice's in here." Dracanna dug through the largest pile of clothes that lay up against the far wall. "Come over here and help me."

"Scoop said to let you know that there are riders coming." Conrad tossed dresses to the side. He began digging in the pile, feeling like he was helping his mother get ready to take her clothes to the cleaners. It hadn't looked like much when they were all hanging on racks, but now, heaped on the floor, with everything else that was going on, the pile felt like more than he could overcome.

"Shit," muttered Dracanna. "Okay, you stay here and find Rice. I'll go out and deal with Genghis and company. As soon as you get her dug out, bring her out front." She turned and left the room. Conrad watched his boss disappear through the door before he went back to digging through the clothes.

It took him another fifteen minutes before he found Rice. The Asian drag queen lay at the bottom of the pile. A pair of small puncture wounds marred the blush on her neck. Blood still oozed from them. Remembering his basic training, Conrad checked her neck for a pulse while careful to avoid the wounds. *No pulse.* He checked for breath. Her silicone-enhanced chest wasn't moving, and no air passed her painted lips. Rice was dead.

***

Dracanna paused to straighten her hair in the mirror

56

over her desk. She had to look her best if she was going to meet the undisputed ruler of this part of space. This wasn't the first time she'd met the Kahn, but he always made her nervous. He suspected Shoppe's power, and he was a man used to getting what he wanted. It wouldn't do for the ship to fall into the dictator's hands, even though Dracanna knew that if Shoppe didn't approve of the 'owner' she wouldn't go anywhere. If something happened to her, Shoppe would go find a new owner, and it would continue to roam the cosmos with Scoop, doing the things that they did, most of which even Dracanna didn't totally understand.

"Bitch, you ain't going to get any prettier." Bea wrung out her mop behind Dracanna. "Go on out there and use your tired charms on the old guy so we can get on with our journey."

Dracanna ignored her. *Everything looks to be in order.* The cow bell on the front door rang with the cheery chime of incoming customers. She pushed her way through the door onto the sales floor. She narrowly avoided Travis as he retreated from the front.

Several guards passed through the doors before the Kahn did. They scanned the shop with military efficiency.

"I am safe here," Genghis's rough voice preceded him through the door. "Neither my good friend Dracanna nor Rice Pilaf would allow anything to happen to me in this establishment." The undisputed ruler of the Mongolian sector sauntered into the Scary Queen.

Of all the rulers Dracanna had ever met, Genghis Kahn was one of the least pompous. He carried himself with power and had an air of forcefulness around him, but he never assumed people knew who he was, at least not in the ice cream shop. His clothes, being little more than riding leathers, weren't any more elaborate than those of his men.

The hilt of his sword had a few more jewels on it than his guards'. But other than that, he looked like any other citizen of Mongoleon: short and dark with almond-shaped eyes and almost yellow skin. Behind the ruler, another servant dragged a pitiful creature. It had a scrawny neck that was emphasized by the ornate bronze collar with a metal chain attached. The large eyes still pleaded as they had every time Dracanna had seen it.

According to legend—after more than two thousand years, it was legend not rumor—even if both parties were still alive—this was the Gray who had captained the spaceship that Genghis commandeered back on Earth. This creature had inadvertently given the Mongol leader the power to overthrow planets and takeover this arm of the galaxy. *No matter how often I see it, I will always feel sorry for it. It looks more pitiful than normal.*

"How may I serve the Kahn today?" Dracanna gave a slight bow. She didn't need to— being on good terms with rulers was something she prided herself on— but a little courtesy went a long way in maintaining good terms.

"Where is the sweet Rice Pilaf?" Genghis smiled.

"We've had a bit of turbulence on the way to Mongoleon and she's helping clean up in the back," Dracanna replied. *I wish she'd get her little oriental ass out here.*

"That's a shame." A slight frown marred his expressive face. "She is such a charming creature."

"That she is."

"It has been too long since your establishment has graced our planet," Genghis continued. His brown gaze darted across the ice cream in the case. "I was beginning to think that we had done something to upset you, Dracanna."

"Oh never, my Kahn." She managed to blush. "We

have just been busy in other sectors of space."

"How long will you be on my most humble of worlds?"

"I don't know at this point. As I said, we hit some turbulence on our way here this time. We may need some repairs before we can depart."

"Anything I have is yours," he said with a lecherous grin. "As long as I get to sample your wares."

Dracanna blushed and batted her long eyelashes at the ruler with a soft giggle. "You know you can always sample my wares." He was one of the biggest flirts in the galaxy. He'd been trying to get her into his harem for centuries, and she'd been artfully dodging him the whole time.

His deep laugh filled the shop. His guards stared off watchfully into space, observing everything that went on. The Gray cringed. Dracanna knew its hearing was different from humans. And it must've either found the particular frequency of the Kahn's laugh painful, or had difficult memories associated with the laugh.

"Do you still have some of that special Ginger Horse-Cream Surprise I so love—almost as much as your company?"

She shook her dark head. "Unfortunately, not at the moment. It was one of the casualties of the turbulence," Dracanna lied. It was only something she made when she knew they would land on Mongoleon. She'd have to whip some up quickly. *I hope I have everything I need for it.* "If you'd like, I can bring some by in a little while after I whip up a new batch."

A twinkle appeared in Genghis's brown eyes as he leered at her. "That would be perfect. Time it for dinner. We shall throw a special feast in your honor, since it has been so very long since you graced my table with your beauty."

"Why Kahn, that would be too much."

"Nonsense. You must come. Close up your shop and bring Rice and anyone else that travels with you. I insist."

Blood drained from Dracanna's face. She never liked leaving Shoppe alone, but she dared not anger Genghis Kahn if she wanted to return to this sector of the galaxy. *There are several special ingredients I can only get from the planets in this region. I have to keep him happy.*

"Of course we'll be there. Is there anything you would like now?"

He shook his dark head. "No, I think not for me." He turned to the men behind him. "Any of you want anything? I'm sure Dracanna would be willing to put it on my tab."

Inside she cringed. *I don't like giving too much away.* Genghis didn't have a tab exactly. He expected free treats whenever she passed through as part of her tribute to him for giving her free rein to move about his domain as she saw fit. She had special arrangements with his accountant. She charged things to his account when shopping in the market in Genghis.

The two guards at the door came forward first, quickly making choices that Dracanna filled. Then the Gray and its handler stepped forward.

"Do you want something, Gyre?" Genghis asked of the Gray.

It nodded its large hairless head. "Some apple, p-p-please, m-m-my Lord." The voice was as sexless as the Gray, but it was weak and shook slightly.

"Some apple then, for Gyre, if you would."

Luckily, the Apple Avalanche had frozen back to a scoopable state. Dracanna severed a cone full of the green treat to the little alien. She felt its hands shake as it took the cone from her. Something broke inside her each time she served the little creature. She wanted to find some way of helping it out of its bondage to the barbarian star lord.

***

"Conrad where are you?" Travis called from the backroom.

Conrad shook and forced himself to stop staring at Rice's body. He'd seen dead bodies before—back in the Middle East—but they had always been the bodies of strangers and there had always been more blood. *Where is all the blood? I've never known the body before. Other than grandfather, at his funeral. But funerals are different. The bodies are cleaned and dressed. Made presentable. What are we going to do with Rice? Even if she was a bit of a bitch, she was a coworker and might've become a friend. We need to tell Dracanna.*

"In the dressing room," he replied.

"How bad is the mess in there?" Bea came through the door before Travis. "I really hope we can find me some new nails."

"I think we have a bigger problem than broken nails," Conrad said.

"I know you're just a baby drag queen, sweetie," Bea bobbed her head around, making her red curls bounce dramatically, "but there are no problems bigger than broken nails... except maybe running mascara."

"Rice is dead."

"Rice is what?" Travis entered behind Bea.

"Did you just say Rice is dead?" Bea asked. Her voice dropped several octaves for a moment.

Conrad stood from where he knelt next to the rapidly cooling body. He gestured toward their coworker. "Yes. I found her under this pile of lame. What do we do?"

"Well first, we don't tell the Kahn. She was his

61

favorite server." Bea stepped toward the body. "Cat, you need to run up front and take over for Dracanna. Tell her we need her back here, but if Genghis is still there, don't tell her why until he leaves. Travis, you can be a dear and help me get all this cleaned up." She stared down at Rice and shook her head. "Poor thang, she always did love lamé but lamé just never loved her. Now it looks just fabulous." Bea made a choking sound and covered her mouth with her large hand.

Conrad looked at Travis and shrugged before he headed out the door. He nearly made it across the backroom before Dracanna rushed in from the front.

"We need horse milk," she announced.

"Uh Dracanna, we have something more pressing than horse milk," Conrad said. He glanced through the closing door to see the short broad backs of men in leather armor walking out. "I found Rice in the dressing room. She's dead."

"Dead?" Dracanna looked indignant. "People don't die in my shop." She pushed past Conrad and stormed into the dressing room.

Conrad followed. *I bet Travis and I will be the ones to carry the body wherever she wants it.* Travis was taking clothes from Bea as she put them on hangers.

"Where is Rice?" Dracanna demanded. She stopped and stared at the body. "How did this happen?"

"If you look at her neck, there's a couple of bloody wounds there," Conrad stepped next to the storekeeper and pointing at the corpse.

Dracanna squatted down and reached her talon-like hand for the body. She sat there for a minute or so staring at the wound, before straightening up.

"How did another vampire get on board?"

***

Conrad looked at the list of things they needed. Dracanna's perfect script spelled everything out, even down to local terms for measurements. Genghis' market was the strangest place he'd ever been. Obviously a bustling hub of activity, both local and extra-planetary, it still looked like an old-time market. There weren't any big gleaming buildings. Hide tents and haggling were the way the people did things. There were all sorts of transportation from horses and other riding beasts to gleaming hover cars and even one jet pack.

"Wow, I've missed this place," Bea said at his side.

"You've been here before?" Travis's blue eyes widened.

"Lots of times," the big drag queen replied. "This is one of Dracanna's normal stops as she tours the galaxy."

"But how can she be touring the galaxy when the shop is on the same corner every day, and has been for...what...at least the three years I've been back?" Conrad tore his eyes away from the brightly-colored cloth for sale in the shop in front of them.

"That's the fun of time travel, my dear," Bea said with a smile. "You can go anywhere, anytime and still make it home in time for dinner, or in this case, in time to open for business."

"How long have you been traveling with Dracanna?" Travis asked.

Bea got a faraway look. "Now, let's see. That's where time travel gets a bit tricky. I started working for her back when I was about twenty. I just turned sixty, two months ago. So, I guess that comes up to forty years, give or take a couple lost here and there."

"Wow, you're sixty?" Travis gawked. "I figured you were about thirty or so, but it's hard to tell under all the makeup."

"My dear boy, you flatter me." Bea giggled slightly and shielded her mouth as she tucked her head demurely. "It's more an effect from the time travel than anything. My body stopped knowing what time was, and I stopped aging."

"So, how old is Dracanna?" Conrad still tried to wrap his mind around the idea that the old woman running the shop was older than she appeared. *How many trips through time before I stop aging?*

"Oh honey, don't ask me, and *do not* ask her." Bea glanced around nervously. "You know she's had work done. Beyond that, she's got her secrets that are not mine to reveal. Let's just say, don't be surprised if you never learn everything there is to know about our boss. She's a lot more than she appears."

Even in the heat of the open-air market, Conrad shivered. "Not sure I want to know all her secrets."

Something behind him caught Bea's eye. "Wow, I've got to see that. Why don't you two go about finding the items on the list? Remember to use the voucher that Dracanna gave you to get the stuff. Most of it should be over at the main market tent—that big one over there." She pointed to a peak of brown leather poking up above the shorter tents. "If I haven't caught up by the time you get everything, head back this way, and I'll find you. Dracanna won't mind if you pick up a little something for yourself while you're at it. I mean, you can't visit somewhere like this and not pick up a souvenir the first time." Bea smiled as she swished into a shop selling brightly-colored clothing and cloth.

Keeping the high tent peak in view, Conrad and Travis found themselves abandoned in the strange market. All around them people moved. Most of them looked like Asian people from Earth, but here and there, other species milled around with the humans.

"Wow, is that a Gray?" Travis pointed at the little alien with the large head and huge dark eyes.

"Don't point," Conrad snapped. He tried to remember what he'd been taught in the Air Force about dealing with other cultures. "We don't know if that's rude or not."

"Sorry," the cowboy replied sheepishly. "This is a lot to take in."

Watching a strange insectoid chittering with a shopkeeper, Conrad just nodded and tried to keep walking toward the main market tent. The odd sea of unusual people closed in around him.

***

"We've got to get the internal sensors back online," Dracanna snarled at Scoop. "Where did we pick up another vampire?"

"How should I know?" he replied. "Something caused that gravity tilt earlier. Have you checked for another ship docked to ours? If it docked while we were tumbling through spacetime, it might've caused our gravity to realign with its gravity, thus causing our tilt."

"Then we need sensors even more." Dracanna tapped on several holographic keys above the ice cream display.

"If there is another ship docked to us, that would explain why we stabilized even without the raspberry crème table."

"Who'd be docking with us?"

"It looks like Rice was killed by a vampire. Could it be a relative of yours?"

"I've had no contact with my family—or anyone from my world—in a very long time. Does Shoppe have anything to say about it?"

"You know Shoppe doesn't like being on

Mongoleon," Scoop replied. "She's being very quiet right now—not even a little indication of what's going on."

Dracanna slapped through the holographic display across the door to the ice cream counter. It flickered for a second. The outline of the shop appeared, then it fuzzed out again. She pulled out a console from under the counter, made a few adjustments, and the screen shimmered back to life. The holographic projection showed a perfect rendition of the shop and a strange leech-like protuberance coming off the side adjacent to the dressing room.

"Looks like we do have an unauthorized ship attached to our side," she said. "Do you want to come along?" She turned off the holographic controls with a swipe of her hand.

"Sure, like I need *more* excitement right now."

***

Conrad stared at the massive tent. They strolled past the last of the smaller tents around it. A large variety of transportation stood around the outside, almost like a parking lot. Amazingly, there wasn't a lot of dust. Most of the dry desert dirt had been packed to a rocky hardness. Horses were hitched to posts next to floating motorcycle-like things and a number of beasts that he couldn't even begin to name.

"I wonder what one of these things would be like to ride?" Travis stared at a huge thing that looked more like a bear than a horse. A small leather patch, that could only be a saddle, sat just behind the thing's prominent hump. Heavy straps of bright-green material were wrapped around the beast's head, tying it off to the hitching post.

Conrad looked at the beast and frowned. "I've got nothing against bears, but I don't think I want to try riding that thing. I don't think it would be very smooth. I rode a camel once in the Middle East, and it wasn't pleasant when

66

you kicked it up to anything faster than a walk. This thing looks like it might be worse."

"You were military." Travis turned his attention away from the bear thing. "You must've traveled a bit and had a much more interesting life than I have. This is the first time I've been outside Texas."

"And this is nothing like anything I've seen on Earth." Conrad shook his head. "I wasn't in the Air Force long—only one deployment. I got lucky and never saw combat, just the occasional aftermath. I was stationed in Saudi for a year. Made a couple of trips through Afghanistan though. That was enough for me."

"But isn't this cool?" Travis asked. "How often do you get to travel to other worlds? Yeah, it's a bit odd, but it's really cool. Like something out of the movies or TV."

Conrad sighed, trying to figure out his real feelings about their situation. "I guess. I wasn't expecting anything stranger than working in an ice cream shop while wearing a dress and wig. This does kinda make that look normal." When he pushed aside the strangeness of all of it, and let Travis's enjoyment influence him, he found himself seeing things through more amazed eyes.

Travis laughed and reached for Conrad's hand. "Come on. Let's go see what they've got in here. You still have the list and the voucher, right?"

He didn't reply at first. Holding Travis's hand felt good. The cowboy's enthusiasm for their strange situation was almost comforting. Conrad wondered for a second if they'd be making this connection so fast if they were back on Earth.

A small alien that looked like a cross between a Gray and a Chinaman came out of the market swinging a backpack onto its narrow shoulders. He—Conrad assumed it was a he—walked over to the bear creature, untied it, jumped up on the saddle and kicked it into a run.

Travis laughed. "See, that just looked cool. I might be a bit big for it though."

"Maybe not. I take it you like the idea of riding bears?" As soon as he said it, Conrad groaned inwardly. *I can't believe I just said that. Maybe I can go crawl into a tent somewhere and just forget about it. We need to keep moving.* "Let's go in and see what they have inside." Conrad pulled Travis' hand to get him moving again once the bear rider disappeared onto the crowded roadway.

The tent's front stood open with the huge flaps pulled back, allowing the warm breeze access to the building's interior. A variety of bins and racks stretched before them as they passed into the shadowed area under the tent top. Conrad paused to let his eyes adjust from the brightness outside.

"How can I be of assistance?" A short Asian woman asked in perfect English.

Dracanna had them eat a special treat she pulled out of a freezer in the back. She said there were special ingredients in it that would allow them to understand any tongue they encountered and be able to speak it as well. The cold concoction wasn't the best tasting thing Conrad had ever eaten, but the minty aftertaste hadn't been too bad. While they consumed the stuff, Bea explained that Shoppe had translated for the Mongolians that had stopped by earlier, but she wouldn't be able to help them out in the market. The effects of the treat would wear off every year or so, and they'd need another round if they were still traveling with Dracanna at that time. It was nice that they had been correct.

"We have a list." Conrad pulled out the paper

Dracanna sent with them. As she accepted the list, he couldn't see anything about the woman that wasn't human. She could have been working on any shop in Chinatown in San Francisco. It made things not quite so strange for him.

"We have most of these items," she said. She then turned and led them deeper into the establishment. "This bears the seal of Dracanna. You work for her?"

Conrad nodded. "Yes, we just landed and need a few supplies."

"I will inform my friends of your arrival." The clerk smiled. "We all enjoy the treats at the Scary Queen when she visits. It's been too long."

The clerk hurried them along, pausing at various bins to select items on the list. At one, where she was selecting some kind of strange melon that was covered with purple splotches, she tisked a bit while digging through the fruit.

"Only the best for Dracanna." She finally selected one and placed it in the basket she'd slung over her arm.

Behind them, a scream tore through the conversational undertones.

"What was that?" Conrad asked as more screams joined the first one. Then a loud roar filled the air. People fled the market in a mad rush, more than a few of them were yelling.

"This is no good," the clerk assisting them said.

"What's not good?" Conrad looked toward the back of the market.

Something came thundering around the fruits and vegetables. Produce and other products went flying. A mass of strawberries scattered across the floor.

"Stampede!" The clerk dropped the basket of goods she'd collected. The melon, fruits, and a bottle of horse milk rolled onto the floor as she fled.

***

Dracanna paused at the wardrobe door in the dressing room. The door doubled as one of many airlocks in the shop. A small panel inside the wardrobe indicated that a ship was indeed docked on the other side. A quick glance at the registry showed it was from Darkholme, Dracanna's home world, but she didn't recognize the registered name of the pilot. Within a couple of taps on the panel, she opened a communications link between her and the ship.

"This is Dracanna, captain of the Scary Queen. Please identify yourself and explain why you have attached yourself to my ship without prior authorization," she said forcefully, knowing it would carry into the docked ship.

No reply came.

"Dracanna, you might want to turn around," Scoop whispered.

With a sigh, she turned back to the dressing room. A tall pale man with long black hair stood in the doorway to the backroom. He wore a perfectly tailored tuxedo and held a top hat in his left hand. There was a spot of blood in the right corner of his pale lips. His bearing and appearance were, without a doubt, Darkholmian. Dracanna didn't recognize the man, but by the way he looked at her, he knew who she was. *I hate it when people know me, but I don't know them. It always makes for awkward conversations.*

***

A surging mass of sturdy mountain ponies charged through the confines of the market tent. Racks of clothing, shelves of wares, and bins of produce didn't deter the terrified equines from their need to run away from something. The horrified herd filled the tent with a seething mass of sweaty horseflesh.

Conrad ran after the clerk, then remembering Travis,

70

he slowed down.

"Right behind you!" the cowboy shouted. "Keep moving!"

Resuming his rapid pace, Conrad made for the bright sunlight shining outside the tent. Ahead of him, a small child slipped and fell. He stopped to pick up the kid.

"Got your back!" Travis shouted as the terrified herd overtook them.

Conrad looked over his shoulder and Travis had pulled off his hat and was waving it around shouting. "Yeahaw ponies! Get along there little guys!" Like a rock in the stream, he stood between Conrad, the child, and the flood of horseflesh. Somehow, all the ponies opted to go around the tall Texan while the child clung to Conrad and screamed for its mother. As the dust and cacophony cleared, Conrad looked around at the chaos the ponies left in their wake.

"I wonder what caused that." Travis said, slipping his hat back on his head.

"Bold!" a woman screamed. The child in Conrad's arms squirmed.

"Mama!"

Conrad set the child down and it ran toward its mother as fast as its chubby little legs could carry it. The mother scooped him up and cooed to him while she walked to the two Earthlings.

"Thank you for saving little Bold!" The mother wrapped her arms around Conrad.

He awkwardly returned the woman's embrace. "It was the least we could do. We couldn't let the ponies run him over."

"You are brave enough to be some of the Kahn's men." She released Conrad.

An angry roar came from the carnage that had been the market tent. Then the tent top tore away allowing the hot desert sun to blaze down into the remains while a giant winged reptile waddled through the wreckage. Its massive green head looked about for something.

Conrad stared. "What in the hell is that?"

***

"So Lord Dragon, you actually went so far as to change your sex to avoid your people," the man facing Dracanna said with a grimace. "There has been talk throughout the great house of Darkholme, but most thought it just idle gossip."

"Who are you, and why are you here?" Dracanna asked trying to be calm. Anger seethed in her, but it wouldn't do to let it boil over.

"Would you be pleased to know your father sent me to find you?" He set his black-velvet top hat on a dressing table. "My name is Wren of the house Wyvern."

"Are you the one who killed my employee?" she snarled, stepping away from the wardrobe.

"If that is what you call an employee, yes." The man looked down at the now covered body of Rice Pilaf. "She wasn't very tasty, but I injured myself when I docked with your ship. It appeared you were out of control and in need of assistance. I figured she was but cattle for your needs."

"Cattle?" Scoop screamed at the man. "She was a living breathing person until you killed her!"

"Oh, you have talking toys." Wren looked down his nose at Scoop. "I lost my interest in those trinkets years ago."

Sputtering in Dracanna's hand, Scoop shook with fury. The only time he could make a physical display of emotion was times of anger, and then it was limited to

72

shaking.

"Scoop is not a toy." Dracanna ignored the utensil's rage. "He is a good friend of mine who had a tragic accident—not unlike poor Rice. Luckily, I was there to help save at least part of him. Now, you can tell me what it is that my father wants with me and then get off my shop."

"It is time for you to come home, Lord Dragon," Wren said. "Your father is gravely ill, and his house is in chaos."

"You think I care about that?" she snapped. *Father, the Grand Lord Dragon, turned his back on me centuries ago. He never understood who I really am. All he ever saw was the stallion to breed the next generation.*

"I really don't care what you care about," Wren said. "I have my orders. If I have to, I will tow this vessel and everyone aboard back to Darkholme as I was instructed. I am authorized to use any force necessary—short of killing you—to achieve my goals. There is nothing in my orders about any of your *employees*." Distaste colored his stress on the word. "I can kill them, or leave them trapped in this barbaric sector of space if they don't come along peacefully."

***

Conrad grabbed Travis' hand to run. The huge reptile thundered through the remains of the market tent toward them. It seemed focused on them. Once clear of the tent, it spread its massive mottled wings. A hot breeze wafted over them, carrying the scent of death and decay.

"No clue what that is," Travis responded.

"Run!" the child's mother screamed. She clutched her offspring to her chest as she took off. Ahead of her, the vast market emptied rapidly.

The giant reptile roared as it ran after them, its heavy

footfalls shaking the ground. Conrad didn't bother looking behind them. He just ran. He knew if they slowed down even a bit, the thing would either crush them with its gigantic feet or scoop them up in its monstrous maw. *Just let us get back to the Scary Queen so we can go back home. I don't care if I ever leave Texas again, as long as we survive the next couple of minutes.*

"This way!" Travis yanked Conrad's arm hard enough to nearly topple him as they ran around one of the tents left intact after the stampede. "No straight lines!"

Conrad wondered what the man was talking about, but didn't have the breath to ask. He followed, feeling the ground shake harder. The beast closed in. His heart hammered as Travis yanked them into a tent full of rugs.

The monster tore through the tent after them.

"Why is it chasing us?" Conrad yelled. They ran out the back of the tent following the terrified natives.

"Who knows? Maybe he has issues with gay bois," Travis replied.

They rounded another tent, and there was Bea. The big drag queen stood in the middle of the walkway, looking like a large, demented Annie Oakley with a small strange-looking gun in her large well-manicured hands which still bore one broken nail. Her aim focused above their heads; she didn't even glance at them.

"Get down," she said calmly.

Conrad dropped to the hard-packed earth, pulling Travis down with him. He rolled to look up at Bea. She delicately squeezed the trigger of the gun. A beam of red light shot from the gun's muzzle. It caught the lizard in the head, slicing laterally through it, and neatly bringing the beast to a stop. The thing wobbled, then crashed into a nearby tent.

74

"Are you two alright?" Bea carefully slid the gun back into her hand bag.

Conrad stood and offered Travis a hand up. "Yeah, nothing broken," he huffed. His breath still coming in short gasps.

"Fine," Travis dusted off his tight jeans.

"I wonder how this got into the city." Bea walked toward the dead lizard. "You know, while we're here, I might just have to see about having a couple of belts and bags made out of this thing. Souvenirs."

"How long are we going to be here?" Conrad looked at the carcass in wonder. With a closer look, it appeared to be some kind of dinosaur with nonfunctioning wings. *But dinosaurs didn't have six limbs. This just gets stranger and stranger.*

"Depends on how long it takes to get the shop fully functioning again. We've got to see if we can find someone to make us a replacement raspberry crème table. That could take a few days, long enough to get this boy skinned, worked over, and tastefully recreated into something functional."

City guards descended on them with all the efficiency of any big-city police department. It took a while to get a cleanup crew to remove the body while merchants around the bazaar hurried to repair their tents and reassure their customers that everything was going to be alright.

Conrad and Travis stood by watching in awe until the clerk from the main market appeared with a bag for them.

"Here are the items from your list," she said thrusting the bag into Conrad's hand. "Thank you both for saving the child. That was very brave. If you need anything while you are here in Genghis, please come by, and if we don't have it, we will find it for you. Also tell Dracanna that I will be sending customers to her tomorrow. She has dinner with the Kahn tonight."

Taking the bag, Conrad couldn't think of anything to say other than. "Thank you very much."

The store clerk bowed to him then hurried off back in the direction of her tent.

"Wow, that was really nice of her," Travis said.

Bea returned from her latest talk with the folks hauling away the lizard's body. "You'll find that people around here tend to be very polite and nice. Apparently, since I'm the one who killed it, I get a say in what happens to the body. We'll all get matching bags, belts, and even boots for the cowboy here. How's that for souvenirs? They're sending the meat over to the homeless shelter."

"They have homeless around here?" Conrad watched a floating crane lift the carcass into the air. *Why would they have homeless when they had science that allowed cranes to float around on a cushion of air?*

"Sweetie, there are homeless all over the galaxy," Bea replied. "Some are just better off than others. So, one of the guys said that someone cut the perimeter fence near the stockyards. They were having their annual pony sale today and the sabersaur came right through causing the stampede. Now, the authorities trying to figure out who cut the fence and why."

Conrad stared at his last sight of the sabersaur as it was carried down the hard-packed sand street. *Is this just bad timing?*

4
Ginger Horse Crème Surprise

"**What** are you going to do about your people?" Scoop asked

"Which people?" Dracanna snarled, dumping chunks of ginger into the swirling mass of crème in the mixing bowl in front of her. "My employees are going to be fine. I'll make sure of that."

"I was talking about your planet."

"My planet can go to hell! They never cared about me, and you know that."

If Scoop had a head, he would have nodded. "Well, I believe you should think on it for a while. It's not like your father asks for help every day."

The next chunks of ginger into the mixing bowl hit a little harder than it should have, sending horse milk splashing up into Dracanna's face. "Damn it Scoop! I'm done with those bloodsuckers, and you know that! It'll take a lot more than one little puissant messenger from my father to get back in my good graces. If I'm lucky, that idiot from House Wyvern will stay locked in the backup freezer until we're ready to leave, then I can dump him and his ship in the nearest star as we pass by." She'd managed to overpower the other Darkholmian by breaking a mirror over his over-fluffed head and then depositing him in the cryo tube in the far back room. *It's better than he deserves, after killing poor Rice. I should've killed him on the spot. I'm from house Dragon and he's just a lowly Wyvern. But we Darkholmians are hard to kill. I'm better off throwing him in a star.*

The door going into the front of the shop opened and Bea Mann walked in. "So, are you going to have that ready in time for dinner with the Kahn?"

Dracanna turned and fixed her employee with a steely gaze that would have made Scoop quiver. "If it's not, then I'll let you entertain the man until it is."

"Now you know, I like my men on the rough side." Bea wagged one of her recently-glossed red nails. "But from what I remember of yurt gossip, I think that man plays a little too rough even for me. And how would he handle my dick being bigger than his?"

"Then leave me alone, so I can finish this!" Dracanna said. "As it is, I'm going to have to use the flash freezer to get it done." The advanced tech of the flash freezer would finish the ice cream off faster than any Earth technology.

"Fine, I'll just go see how the bois are doing." Bea turned and walked across the backroom toward the dressing room.

***

"I don't understand why I have to wear this thing," Conrad held up the thick woolen skirt that Bea had dug out of her shopping bundles when they returned to the shop.

"Hey, I feel like a clown in this," Travis complained, turning around in the billowing brown pants he'd been given.

"At least those are men's clothes." Conrad tossed

Travis the matching light-weight tunic. It seemed a shame for the man to cover up his massive, nearly-perfect chest, but they needed to finish getting ready. Dracanna had said something about not having much time before the Kahn's men would arrive to escort them all to dinner.

Travis caught the tunic. "They still feel strange."

"The Kahn likes his guests to honor the local traditions," Bea strolled into the room. "Oh don't put that away on my account." She smiled and gestured toward Travis's chest. He quickly pulled the tunic on. It hung down past his knees. "How are you two coming? Her Bitchiness out there isn't going to be happy if we're not all ready in time."

Conrad glared at the skirt. "If I could figure out how this thing goes on, I might be ready."

"Oh, deary. Here, let Auntie Bea help you." The drag queen's large hands moved deftly as she assisted Conrad in getting into the strange costume. Luckily, the Mongolian skirt was a lot easier to wrap than it looked like.

"I still don't understand why I have to wear girls' clothes for this," Conrad complained as Bea slid the sparkling, flower-appliqué blue blouse over his head. All the bead work on the blouse added weight that he didn't expect.

"You're one of Dracanna's employees," Bea explained "You'll find that on some planets, that gives you a certain prestige and more than a few protections. Everyone around here knows that only drag queens work for the Scary Queen. We can pass Travis off as your man—"

"But I'm not his man," Travis interrupted as he wrapped the wide yellow sash that went with the brown costume around his narrow waist. He caught Conrad's eye and smiled. "Yet."

Bea grinned wickedly and plopped a long dark wig on

Conrad's head before she continued. "That's for the two of you to decide. But if everyone thinks you're an employee's man, you'll be safer. The two of you earned some favor in the Kahn's court today by saving that little boy from the stampede. To some people, that won't be a good thing. Keep that in mind. Being attached to the store will give you protection you wouldn't have if you were just a traveler."

Travis gulped. "Everyone seems so friendly."

"Because they know you're with the shop, more specifically, with Dracanna. While she's in favor with the Kahn, we'll be in favor with the people. She works hard to stay in favor with most of the people in charge of the worlds we visit. It makes things easier." Bea handed Conrad a flat hat made of red fox fur with a lot of small beads and bright ribbons dangling from the sides and back.

"What does Dracanna do to win the favor of the rulers?" Conrad asked. He settled the hat over the long dark wig. All total, the ensemble weighed more than the combat helmet he'd had to wear in basic training.

"Oh honey," Bea reached out and helped him get the hat in place. "There are some things that even I don't want to know about. It's been that way since I've been working for Her Bitchiness." She stepped back and looked at Conrad. "At least, for your sake, on this planet the women aren't big into makeup. I swear that more than a few of them look more like men than Travis the cowboy over there does. Well, I think you'll pass for the night. Now let's see what I can find. Just because the women aren't big into makeup, doesn't mean that I don't need to keep mine in tip-top shape."

A soft chime rang through the dressing room.

Bea looked up. "Shit, they're early. Cat Astrophe, go out front and entertain our escort. Travis, go see if you can be of any help to Dracanna. I'll be out in a minute." She shooed the two out of the dressing room.

Conrad swallowed as the door closed behind him. *What am I supposed to do to entertain the men of Genghis Kahn?* He barely glanced at Dracanna, still working on the frozen confection that she was taking for the Kahn. A gut instinct told him to stay as far away from her as possible. *It's almost like something happened while we were gone. She's been even grumpier than earlier. It might just be her doing whatever it was she did to Rice's body.* Rice had vanished by the time they returned from their shopping adventure, but no one had asked Dracanna what happened.

The escort claimed they knew they were early and hoped for a bit of ice cream before setting out for the Kahn's dinner. Luckily, Conrad managed not to drip any ice cream on his outfit as he served up a free round. When he came out front, Travis hovered near the cash register. Conrad couldn't tell if he was trying to look protective or just didn't know what to do. They didn't have long to wait. The three men of their escort had just finished their treats when Dracanna emerged from the back room, looking elegant in a black version of the bright clothes Conrad wore. Bea Mann followed their employer, carrying a huge vat of ice cream. The large redhead was decked out in shades of greens and had added a dark burgundy veil.

"We are ready," Dracanna announced. Just into the dining room, she paused for a moment, then strolled past the Kahn's men heading toward the door.

The guards scrambled up from their table and hurried to reach the door before Dracanna. The first one there swung the door open and bowed slightly as she swept past him and out into the street beyond. Conrad and Travis fell into step behind Bea.

"What's with the veil?" Conrad asked Bea softly as they walked.

"They're optional here," she said with a light chuckle. "I always think a veil adds a layer of mystery to one's façade. Although, now that I think about it, it makes all the work I did on my makeup fairly superfluous. Oh well. It's not every night we dine with Genghis Kahn."

Conrad didn't respond. He just followed along and tried to take in as much of the local scenery as he could.

The market crowd had diminished from earlier in the day, but those still there parted before the line of guards and foreigners. It reminded Conrad of the way people get out of the path of police cars when they have their sirens wailing. All down the dusty street, people stepped to the side. From the tents around them, people peered out. When Conrad looked toward them, tent flaps dropped and people disappeared, or just turned their heads. There were hushed whispers everywhere.

They turned a corner and stepped onto the first stone street Conrad had seen in the city. For a moment, a group of the strange, bipedal insect people openly stared at them. Something in their many-faceted gazes made him uncomfortable.

***

At the end of the stone street sat the largest yurt Conrad had ever seen. Its bright-blue silk sides glistened in the setting sun. The sunlight reflected off the wispy clouds in shades of purple and blue he'd never seen before. Had they not been in the middle of a procession, he would've been tempted to stop and watch for a couple of minutes. But neither their guards nor Dracanna showed any signs of pausing for the natural beauty.

"It's really cool." Travis nodded at the horizon. "I've

never seen anything like it."

"I guess we'll see things like it on alien worlds," Conrad replied in a hushed tone. For the first time, he thought about visiting other worlds and seeing what wonders they had to offer.

The tent flap opened and a short man with dark hair stood there. He appeared to ignore the massive guards in their simple red tunics and black hats. With a strong purposeful stride, he marched over to the party.

"Ah, lovely Dracanna," his accent was thick despite the translator treat Conrad consumed earlier.

"Genghis," Dracanna bowed to the intergalactic leader. "I can't express my pleasure at dining with you tonight."

"It is the least I can do." The ruler nodded his head. "My table is always graced by your beauty." He glanced around, looking past Conrad, Travis and the guard that brought up the rear of their procession. "Please come in." he turned and motioned them all to follow him into the massive yurt.

They walked into an opulent palatial space that appeared twice the size of the yurt. They strolled down a plush golden carpet toward a gigantic low-sitting table surrounded by many-colored cushions. Gold and silver ornaments sparkled in the harsh light cast by huge glowing orbs that looked like captured minute suns floating near the ceiling. Amid all the grandeur, an oppressive feeling settled over Conrad. *Something's wrong here.* More food than he'd ever seen on a table rested before them. He couldn't identify most of it, other than animal, vegetable and questionable. Somewhere nearby unseen drums beat a soft steady rhythm.

Genghis Kahn proceeded to the head of the table. He gestured for Dracanna to take the cushion to his left. Down the table to his right, a number of beautiful women sat. *These must be his harem.* Further down the table on their side, starting next to Travis, other people stood apparently waiting for something to happen.

In a brilliant, gold cage behind the Kahn, a small gray alien stood. Its large head was bowed so Conrad couldn't make out details of its face.

"I do not see the fair Rice among your entourage this evening," the galactic dictator observed. He paused for a moment, and seemed to be watching the gathered diners before sitting down on the cushion and indicating that the others should as well.

Dracanna settled into her place. "It seems she was more injured than I first thought in our turbulence in getting to Mongoleon. It could be several days or longer before she is well enough for visitors."

Conrad sat down between Bea and Travis after Bea placed the tub of ice cream in the center of the table. It looked like someone had purposely left a place there for the dessert. He remembered what Bea had said early about not wanting to tell the Kahn about Rice's death. *Will we be able to stop him from finding out?*

"Please convey my sympathies to my dear Rice and tell her I expect to see her as soon as she is well enough. My life is lessened without her beauty."

Dracanna nodded solemnly. "All of our lives are lessened without her beauty."

The Kahn stabbed a slice of something that looked like roast beef from the platter in front of him. This appeared to be the signal for the others, none of whom Conrad had been introduced to. All conversation died for a while as people ate their fill. The roast beef was tasty until the Kahn asked them how they enjoyed the lizard they'd brought down earlier in the day. Conrad managed to give a pleasant, wordless reply after a rough swallow to get the last bite down. *Wasn't that supposed to go to the homeless?* After that he stuck with what he presumed were vegetables. All through dinner, the oppressive feeling never lifted.

After the Kahn had eaten his main course, he unceremoniously reached for the ice cream and served himself up a large portion. A grin of delight lifted the corners of his thin dark mustache as he spooned the golden frozen delight into his mouth.

"My dear dear Dracanna," he said between bites. "I cannot express the sheer pleasure I get from consuming the labors of your hands."

"My heart swells with your pleasure." She bowed slightly over her mostly-untouched plate.

Genghis said something else that was too low for Conrad to make out, but Dracanna giggled and demurely slapped his hand. The Kahn laughed as he continued to eat his dessert. Several of the women opposite the Scary Queen employees glared. Further down, people chuckled, but the sound had a distinctly nervous edge to it. Conrad wanted to ask Bea what was going on, but decided to wait until they were back at the shop.

Once the galactic overlord finished his portion of the ice cream, he gestured grandly around the table. People shifted nervously in their seats.

"Please come forth if you would like some of this grand delight," he said. "I find it only fitting to share with everyone this night. I also suggest that everyone stop in and give patronage to the lovely Dracanna while she is here in Genghis. We do not get nearly enough of her very busy time."

Only a couple of the youngest and prettiest women

across from them moved toward the ice cream. After they returned to their cushions, others silently rose and got their dessert. Conrad shivered at the strangeness of it. It was almost like Thanksgiving dinner with no talking, other than one or two soft conversations a short distance from him. The Kahn continued his discussion with Dracanna, but Conrad caught his gazes moving around the room, apparently watching who got up for ice cream and who stayed on their cushion observing silently.

Once everyone returned to their seats, the hidden drum beat grew louder and the women who didn't have ice cream rose and danced around the table. Their heavy skirts floated around them as they spun about. Conrad couldn't help but watch as they moved, twirling and swaying to the drum beats. As they finished their dessert, the younger women rose and joined the older ones, until all the women across from them were dancing.

"They call it the Kahn-Kahn," Bea leaned over and whispered in Conrad's ear.

"I thought the can-can involved kicking," he replied, not quite catching what she said.

The big drag queen gave a deep chuckle. "I didn't say can-can, I said Kahn-Kahn. It's the state dance, but only performed by the Kahn's wives. I think that's one of the reasons Dracanna doesn't want to be part of his harem." Her voice dropped to the point Conrad could barely hear her. "The old bitch couldn't dance to save her life."

Conrad stifled a chuckle and went back to watching the wives dance in swirling color. Even their lively movements couldn't lighten the yurt's oppressive atmosphere. He wanted to get out of there, and back to the safety of the shop. The idea that the little ice cream shop that traveled through time and space was safe gave Conrad pause. *When did I start thinking of the shop as safe? So far nothing that happened to me in or around that place has been safe.* But the atmosphere there was more comfortable to him than this yurt with its strange Asain aliens. He glanced up at the caged Gray. Maybe that was what made him nervous here? The small hunched creature was the thing more than a few horror movies revolved around. It triggered something deep inside him.

The floor beneath his cushion shook. Others must have felt it too, because the dancers stopped moving and looked down with wide terror-filled eyes. Then something resembling the point of a knife sliced through the thick carpet inches in front of his sitting cushion. The massive table shook violently before it shot up into the air.

"What is the meaning of this?" Genghis shouted from the head cushion.

Conrad started to rise, but his cushion shook so hard it knocked him back on his ass. He tried to scramble off it, but it suddenly fell out from under him. Travis's large hand caught his.

"Shit!"

"Hold on." Travis started to pull Conrad out of the hole that appeared under the cushion.

Something hard grabbed hold of Conrad's ankle and yanked him down. He clung to Travis.

"Pull me up!" he shouted. "Something's got a hold on me!" Around the table other people screamed.

"I demand to know what's going on!" the Kahn continued to shout.

Chaos reigned down on his dinner party.

The thing holding on to Conrad yanked hard enough that he felt something pop in his hip. Pain shot through him and he almost let go of Travis. It rekindled the pain in his back. An unbidden scream escaped his lips. More of him slid into the hole.

"Hold on, honey!" Bea shouted from his other side. "Dracanna, do something!"

"Kinda busy right now!" the gravelly voice replied from outside of Conrad's vision.

Travis jerked, losing his balance when the next yank came. Conrad screamed as another round of pain shot through his hip and back. He wanted to cling to the big hand holding him, but he was slipping away with each wave of agony that now coursed through him. He couldn't feel his ankle where the thing held on. Travis's welcome hand was barely a sensation to him. Then, with a final pull from below, the pain became too much. He fell into darkness.

***

Bea's blaster sizzled in Dracanna's ear as the chaos erupted around them. She turned to see Travis's boots disappear down the hole that was quickly closing under where Cat Astrophe had recently sat. A ring of steel appeared around Genghis as his guards sprang to protect their Kahn. Several of the wives disappeared along with two of the other guests.

"What is going on here?" Dracanna screamed at the top of her lungs.

"Defend Dracanna and her people!" Genghis shouted to his guards.

"We need to move all of you to solid ground, my Kahn!" shouted a man that Dracanna recognized as the captain of the guard.

"And two of my people are already gone!" Dracanna snarled as the swords formed around her and Bea.

"This way ladies," the captain said.

The ring of guards began moving awkwardly out of

the yurt. They paused every few feet and glanced around as if making sure that the way was clear. The chaos began dying down as they moved away. No one else around the table disappeared as they stepped through the tent flap out into the quiet night.

"Genghis, what is going on?" Dracanna demanded. She fell into step with the hurrying intergalactic leader.

"Just a little disturbance," Genghis replied, following his guards. "Nothing unexpected."

"Nothing unexpected?" Dracanna didn't try to modulate her tone to something polite. "Two of my people have disappeared. I presume abducted, and you say nothing unexpected! I thought, here in your capital, things were stable."

"You move in circles of power, you know that there are always people waiting to strike when one's guard is down," the Kahn explained. They stopped outside a massive stone building. From the lack of dust, Dracanna knew it was newly constructed. Everything here on Mongoleon quickly developed a thick coating of brown desert dirt. Two guards dashed into the building and quickly returned before the captain ushered them in.

"Go see my remaining wives to their boudoir. Guarantee my guests that I am alive and we will be doing everything possible to find those that were taken."

The captain nodded and rushed out.

Dracanna waited for the heavy metal door to close before she rounded on their host. "We're attacked in your ceremonial yurt by some kind of burrowers and you hurry us off to a newly built concrete bunker. You knew about a possible attack and didn't take proper precautions!"

The Kahn paled under her verbal assault. "We have had a recent series of attacks. Like they're testing my defenses," he confessed. That it came out so easily, told Dracanna that something was indeed wrong, and worrying the man. *Normally he'd be more defensive of someone, even me, getting in his face like this.*

"Like that stampede in the market this afternoon?" Bea tucked her blaster back into her clutch purse.

Genghis nodded. "We have been unable to confirm if that incident was related to the others, but there is a good possibility."

"Do you at least know which group is behind the attacks?" Dracanna fought the urge to pace the sparsely furnished room.

"My dear Dracanna, you know that the more powerful a person is, the more enemies they attract." The Kahn ran a hand nervously through his long black hair.

"So you have no idea who's behind this?" Dracanna snarled.

The intergalactic ruler had the good sense to simply nod.

***

Shoppe quaked in fury, shaking Scoop in his rack on the counter next to the cash register. "What's wrong?" he asked.

The sentient edifice didn't communicate in words, just a series of pictures and feelings. She sent images of Conrad and Travis travelling through darkness. Her fear for them came through as they moved away faster than should've been possible. Then Shoppe tried to take off. The whole place shook, but still missing the one table and only being held in place by the intruder's ship, she couldn't rescue her newest crew members. The lights in the main room dimmed as Shoppe screamed out at their loss.

Scoop lost consciousness from the intensity of her

outcry. It was several minutes later before he struggled back to waking. *Shoppe really likes Conrad. What does she knew about him that she isn't telling the rest of us?*

***

The pain in Conrad's hip was just a dull ache as he opened his eyes to find himself encased in darkness. His back felt fine. It smelled like he had been dipped in a bottle of alcohol. For a second he gagged. He felt for Travis, but the cowboy didn't appear to be there. Somewhere in the distance, a woman screamed. Reaching out, his hands encountered a hard, sticky surface. It reminded him of the unfinished side of a boat one of his Air Force boyfriends had taken him fishing in once. But the boat hadn't been sticky. The screaming continued. He pushed against the surface, and it gave way an inch or so. Conrad tried to move his feet to get better leverage, but something held them in place. Pain lanced through his hip as he squatted down a bit, so he could brace his back against the rear of whatever he was in.

Conrad took a deep breath, forcing himself to ignore the pain. With his back braced the best he could, he put his hands on the rough surface before him and pushed with all his might. His hip complained again as his muscles tightened. His back started aching again, but his hands slid further into the substance imprisoning him. Wondering how thick the stuff was, he continued to push until he felt his fingertips cracked a ridged surface coating the outside. *"Is this what it feels like to break out of the inside of a jelly bean?"* He pushed more of the surface away. *"Or more like a bird hatching?"* Straightening in the dark confines, Conrad turned his mind and hands to breaking off chips of the shell-like surface. With the screaming continuing nearby, he carefully brought what chips he could inside the dark enclosure so he wouldn't make any noise on the outside that his captors could hear. *I can only assume that they're hostile and I need to be as quiet as possible.*

As the hole grew bigger, light seeped into Conrad's confinement. Even with light, the thing reminded him of the fiberglass boat. There were lots of little fibers running along the wall. The capsule-shaped pod was just barely bigger than he was. Glancing down at his feet, he realized the fibers were grown up around them. With his strongest pull, a huge pain spike surged through his hip and back. He couldn't pull free of the fibers. He didn't have the right leverage. The fact that he could move his leg at all, told him that someone had put his hip back in place after they'd dislocated it during the kidnapping.

The screaming stopped. Conrad froze in his efforts to free himself from the egg-like cocoon. The sound of several large feet coming into the room echoed in his confines. Hoping his opening wasn't visible to them, Conrad peered out into the well-lit chamber.

"Who selected the guests to kidnap?" a voice chattered.

"Selected?" another voice replied. "Who said there was a selection? We were just lucky to dig into the royal yurt, grab a couple of people and get out."

"Well that one was useless," the first voice said. "What these humans think they accomplish with all the screaming is beyond me. How could we get any answers out of her when she never stopped screaming? Hopefully she'll be a decent hostage."

"At least she won't be able to scream in the cocoon," the second one added with an odd click.

When they passed through his narrow field of view, they were some of the insect aliens. *Like I saw in the market earlier, except these are larger. Why have they kidnapped people from the Kahn's party? Dracanna said something about Genghis ruling this arm of the galaxy. Maybe the insects aren't happy about that.*

"Which one do you want to try next?" the first one asked. Conrad wished he could see more, but didn't want to risk drawing attention by trying to move his cocoon.

"How about that tall male? One of Dracanna's people."

Silence filled the room for a moment. Conrad's heart skipped a couple of beats. *They have to mean Travis. Don't torture Travis.*

"Do you really want to risk Dracanna's wrath?" the first one broke the silence.

"We have just angered the Kahn more than anyone has dared in over a thousand years. What is the wrath of Dracanna? We already have two of her people," replied the second one. The chittering voice was closer than it had been.

"Kidnapping and ransom are one thing. Torturing him to get information, that's totally different. I've heard rumors of those that have angered the Scary Queen." There was another pause before the he continued. "If you want to see what he knows of the Kahn's plans, be my guest, but give me time to get off planet first."

Conrad wondered what was so scary about Dracanna that these insect-men didn't want to upset her past kidnapping.

"Fine, we'll take the male party guest, the mayor, see what he knows."

A tearing sound filled the room. It raised goose bumps along Conrad's arms, causing the brown hair there to stand on end. Moments later the two insects dragged a man that Conrad recognized from the party past his cocoon and out of the room. Conrad managed to get more of his confinement chipped away before the new round of screaming started.

***

"Insectoids," Dracanna muttered as she straightened from where she inspected the now-small indentations on the soft yurt floor. She turned to the captain of the guard and glared at the man. "How far is the nearest insectoid colony?"

The man looked thoughtful for a moment. "My Lady, we irradiated the Insectoids's hives several generations ago. There are only a few living in our cities. You know how the Kahn feels about genocide."

Dracanna fixed the man with her steeliest gaze. "Yes, I know how the Kahn likes genocide. It looks to me like you have a definite Insectoid problem here. Or at the very least, someone is working with them." *I don't know if we'll ever know how many civilizations Genghis wiped out as he took over this arm of the galaxy. I'm actually impressed that any Insectoids managed to survive, let alone have the balls to show up around here.*

As Dracanna stepped toward the next spot, the one where Cat had been lost, something glistened in the thick torn fibers of the lush carpet. She reached down and the small sparkling object reminded her of a diamond, but was thin and flexible like foil. The captain was looking down at another spot, so Dracanna slipped the piece in her large black shoulder bag. Further inspection of the area turned up no evidence of either Cat Astrophe or Travis.

"Captain," she called to the accompanying guard. "I'm ready to return to my shop."

"But I should escort you back to the Kahn."

"We'll return to the Kahn after you escort me to my shop," she replied sternly.

"The Kahn will not be pleased," the guard objected.

"I'll deal with Genghis." Dracanna smiled, enjoying

the discomfort showing on the captain's face as she used the Kahn's given name. She turned and strolled out of the yurt, and didn't really look to see if the captain followed her or not.

***

Conrad pushed enough of the cocoon away that he was able to see other cocoons lining the walls of the room. *How am I going to find Travis? First I have to free myself.* His hip complained again when he tried to get leverage to free his feet from the strands restraining them. With enough of the front removed, he was able to bend over far enough to awkwardly reach the fibers. Constantly listening for the insects' return, he worked to pull the sticky filaments away enough that he could move his left foot. Ignoring the pain, Conrad, bolstered by the progress, pulled frantically at the fibers around his right foot

He had to smother a cheer, as his right foot came free. Conrad leaned back into the cocoon and took a long breathe to stifle the pain racing up and down his side. He hoped he would be able to walk enough to find Travis, get the cowboy free and then find their way back to the ice-cream shop and get back to Dallas in one piece.

After a couple of minutes, the pain subsided. Conrad listened and there was still no sound of the insects returning. He eased his way out of the cocoon and looked around. Several more cocoons stood around his. They were of various sizes. Based on the height of the inhabitants of Mongoleon, he presumed that the tallest was Travis. He banged on the cocoon hoping that Travis would respond from within. He waited a minute before pounding again. *Still nothing.*

The outside of the cocoon was smoother and harder than the inside had been. Conrad hoped it would crack like an egg so he could get to Travis. He listened for anyone approaching before he struck it as hard as he could. Where his fist impacted the hard surface, lines spider-webbed out. His knuckles throbbed as he drew back for another blow.

From behind, a huge hairy hand closed around his head.

***

Dracanna burst through the doors of the Scary Queen. The intense sadness of the shop struck her. She was never as privy to Shoppe's thoughts as Scoop was, but it was obvious something had upset her panspacial vehicle.

"What's wrong?" she asked, silently hoping that the doors would close behind her, preventing the captain of the guard from following her into the shop. She ignored the man as the door opened behind her.

"You're back!" Scoop said from where she'd left him beside the cash register.

"For a moment," Dracanna snapped as her high heels clicked on the tile floor. "What's got Shoppe upset?"

"Conrad and Travis are missing, aren't they?" Scoop replied.

Dracanna paused. In all her centuries of travelling with Shoppe, she'd never known the vehicle could keep track of the people she carried. *Is there something special about Cat Astrophe that I haven't realized yet?*

"Yes, there was an attack on the Kahn's dinner. They were taken by what I believe was Insectoids," she explained as she approached the counter.

"Who is talking?" the captain demanded.

Dracanna didn't bother turning back toward the man. "I know that the Kahn has conscripted every piece of Gray tech he could get his hands on. Surely that includes artificial intelligence." She didn't feel like explaining the reality of

96

Shoppe and Scoop to the man.

"But our computers respond to us without asking questions," the man replied with a certain level of arrogance.

"Well I prefer mine to be a bit more engaging and with free thought," Dracanna snarled. She swept past the cash register and snatched Scoop out of his holder. "Now if you will excuse me, I need to refresh myself before we return to the Kahn." She didn't wait for a response, but strolled through the door into the back room.

Once the door closed, she walked over to her desk and set Scoop in the holder there. "Now, I need you to run an analysis on this." She pulled the flimsy scrap she'd found out of her purse. And, laid it on the desk in front of the implement. "I think it's Gray tech, but found it where the Insectoid pulled Cat and Travis down."

"If it is modern Gray technology, then it might be resistant to our scans," Scoop replied. "This could take a little while."

"I need to get back to the Kahn," Dracanna replied, pulling out a mirror from a desk drawer. She ran a talon-like hand through her full dark hair. "Bea or I will check back in a while." She looked around the room. "Shoppe, we'll do our best to find them."

"Don't forget we're still short a raspberry crème table," Scoope said as Dracanna rose from the desk.

"Yes the table." She sighed. "Last time I checked there was a craftsman in the bazaar here who could replicate what we need. We're sure there's not one in the storeroom?"

"Shoppe scanned for one, there are shards of the last one but not enough to even pile it in the right spot and get lift off. We could cannibalize the Darkholme ship-"

"Let's not," Dracanna cut him off. "I want to get that pompous lordling out of here when we can. We don't even know if any of the parts over there are compatible with Shoppe. At this point, we're just lucky that Shoppe was able to incorporate it into her façade so that Genghis and his folks don't realize there's another Darkholmian vessel here."

"If there are un-enslaved Grays around, they might be able to detect it," Scoop added.

"Then let's hope there aren't," Dracanna said as her hand closed on the doorknob. "I have managed to stay out of Genghis's conflict with the Grays for years. I mean to keep it that way."

***

"How did you manage to escape the cocoon?" a deep voice grumbled in Conrad's ear as the huge, almost-human hand yanked him against a large hairy body and a thick arm closed around his chest.

He kicked the thing's shin as hard as he could, wishing for the first time that he still had his high heels on. They would've been useful in this situation, making more of an impact than his bare feet did. He jammed his elbow back into the burly ribs as hard as he could.

A heavy ooofff rewarded his efforts, but the arm across his chest tightened.

"Hey, stop that. You're Dracanna's new girl aren't you? I'm a friend."

"I'm not a girl," Conrad replied.

"Well, I guess you guys aren't, but Dracanna and Bea like to be called ladies, so I figured you all did."

Conrad glanced down at the long thick hair of the arm around his chest. "Sassy?"

"The same," the Sasquatch said as he released Conrad.

"How are you talking, and what are you doing here?"

"I bet you ate that translator stuff so you can

98

understand anyone you come in contact with. As for what I'm doing here, well that's a bit more complicated."

Conrad turned and looked up into the big brown eyes. "But back in Dallas you were doing the whole pantomime thing with Bea." *And now I'm standing in the middle of an alien planet having a discussion with a bigfoot after being kidnapped by giant bugs. Yeah, the day just gets weirder.*

Sassy chuckled, a deep rolling chuff. "She likes it. She treats me so nice when I do that. Adds to my mystique, don't you think?"

In the distance, the sound of heavy insect feet echoed from the hallway.

"This could get awkward," Sassy said. He grabbed Conrad and darkness enveloped them.

"Hey," Conrad yelped as the room disappeared.

***

"Well, did you find anything?" Bea asked Dracanna as her employer returned to Genghis's bunker. A short distance away, the Kahn rose from his sturdy camp chair.

Dracanna rubbed her fingers together just enough to let her second in command know that she'd tell her more later. "Not much. Just enough to let me know that Insectoids were behind the attack."

"Nothing we didn't already know," Genghis said standing in front of his wooden bow chair. "I will have every insect in this sector exterminated like we should have when I took over this planet!"

"I can't tell you how to rule your people, Genghis, but I need to save *my* people," Dracanna said, as evenly as possible. "Let me use my contacts and see what I can find out. If you go in with guns blazing, the odds are that the hostages will be killed."

Genghis Kahn frowned, causing his thick black

mustache to sag. "My dear Dracanna, you know how much I value your counsel and the lovely sweet treats. It is only due to this that I shall consider what you propose. Please give me some time to think and decide what is best for my realm." He dismissed them with a wave of his hand. Dracanna bowed slightly before retreating from the bunker with Bea in tow.

After forcing the guard captain on me earlier, he's letting us go a bit too easily, but I'll take what I can get. "We need to speak with that craftsman in the bazaar, the one who can make the tile tables," Dracanna said. "Hopefully, he can get us a replacement table quickly."

"What's up?" Bea asked. "I mean, more than is obvious."

"I think there are Grays involved with the Insectoids," Dracanna said as they rounded the next corner.

"I thought they didn't like each other," Bea said.

"They don't. And if they're working together that means they have something big planned. I want to get Shoppe fixed, Cat Astrophe and the cowboy back, and get off this desert world before it blows sky high."

***

The darkness faded and Conrad found himself standing in the same room he had before the shadows closed in on him. He and Sassy stood there for a moment, listening to the sound of retreating insect feet on the metal floor.

"How ...why did you do that?" he rounded on the Sasquatch.

"Bigfoot secret." The large man smiled. It involved an uncomfortable amount of teeth. "How do you think we manage to avoid you humans seeing us all the time back on Earth? Shadows are our friends and when there aren't any, we make them ourselves."

100

Conrad paused for a moment, thinking about what that meant. It was another thing to add to the list of strangeness for the past two days. *What is life going to be like back in Dallas? There all I have to deal with is the strange old guys hitting on me at the bars while I worry about how I'm going to pay my bills. The longer this goes on, the more normal it becomes. Regular jobs are going to be boring. Even in the Air Force I wasn't kidnapped by insect people while on a strange alien world. I was just a simple clerk. If this is really interesting, I need to work up the courage for some changes in my life, and soon.*

Forcing the thoughts out of his head, he squared his shoulders. "We need to find Travis and get out of here."

"He's in the big one that you were working on cracking," Sassy said. "So tell me, how did you escape the cocoon?"

Conrad walked over to Travis's damaged prison. "I chipped away at it from the inside."

"That's the thing, when the Insectoids cocoon someone, they inject you with a neurotoxin excreted from their stingers that paralyze their victim so that they remain calm while wrapped up."

Conrad pounded on Travis's cocoon. "Not sure what to tell you. Maybe I got a light dose or something." He didn't really care how he got out. The important thing was that he had escaped his confinement.

Sassy looked thoughtful for a moment before he grabbed Conrad's hand. "Let me." He pulled his arm back and shattered the cocoon in the spot where Conrad had struck it several times already. Travis slumped inside the cocoon. His rugged face was slack and his blue eyes were closed.

"Travis, wake up," Conrad said reaching in and

shaking the broad shoulders.

"We'll either have to find some antidote, or wait for it to wear off." Sassy pushed past Conrad. He reached in and ripped the strands holding the cowboy's boots to the bottom of the cocoon. "It amazes me that they use this stuff on folk's feet. I guess they think it holds them upright. Let's get him out of here. We'll get you guys back to the Scary Queen so Dracanna can get you back to Earth where you belong." He heaved Travis out of the cocoon.

"What are you doing, Sasalmater?" an Insectoid voice clicked behind them.

Conrad spun around. Four Insectoids stood there. Two leveled large guns at them. The other two stood there with a Mongolian man supported between them.

***

"You've got to be kidding me!" Dracanna tossed a table at the terrified little Mongolian man standing before her. "I've been buying tables from your family for several generations."

The little man bowed. "And my family has always been humbled by the presence of the most magnificent Dracanna in our establishment. Your patronage has brought much esteem to our business."

"Then why are you not going to be able to make me the new table that I need?" The man's messenger had arrived as she and Bea were trying to find Cat and Travis. She wasn't in the mood to deal with his incompetence. The longer they delayed getting off world, the more chance there was they would to end up in the middle of the conflict between Genghis and whomever was plotting against him.

"The special clay we use in the creation of your tables was declared a controlled substance by his highness shortly after your last visit. We would be most happy to make your table if you bring in the proper permits."

Dracanna glared down her beak-like nose at the man. "And why didn't you tell Bea this when she placed the order for the table several hours ago?"

"I must offer my most humble apologies, gracious lady, but it was my assistant who spoke to your worker. It was not until I looked at the order that I realized the problem. Again, I offer my most humble apologies."

"So, once I get Genghis to sign off on this, how long will it take to get my table made? Actually let's make that two tables. I might as well have a replacement."

"Once the Kahn issues the order, with my current backlog, it could take two weeks."

Dracanna's black nails dug grooves into the shiny tile of the counter that separated her from the merchant. Around the sharp dark points, the tile cracked with an ear-wrenching squeal. "I'll pay double my regular price to move my order up to the top of your list, or I will find another person in another quadrant of space to make what I need from now on." She'd been dealing with this family since her escape from Darkholme nearly fifteen hundred years earlier. But there were other people who could make what she needed. If she was forced to go back to Darkholme, she could get one there. *But there, I'll be dealing with father's whims. Somehow I doubt they'll be much better than Genghis'.*

"Yes gracious lady, for double the regular price, we would most happily create anything you need, as quickly as possible."

"I doubt you could turn my shop into an intergalactic battle cruiser," she muttered as she turned to leave the store. She paused at the tent flap that opened onto the busy market. "Start your preparations. I'll be back with permission for you to make what I need." *I doubt I have to guess why*

Genghis has made the clay a restricted substance. He's hoping that I'll reveal something to either himself or the table maker about the process of crafting Shoppe's components. They have so little understanding of how it all works, or the fact that the clay for the tables is just part of the equation, a major component, but still just a part. And I'm not about to give him the knowledge he needs to replicate all of it.

***

"Sasalmater, why do you have the minions of Dracanna out of their cocoons?" the Insectoid with the gun asked.

Conrad's heart pounded as Sassy paused. He really didn't want to end up with his brains splattered all over the strange metallic room blasted by an Insectoid on a world ruled by Genghis Kahn. He wanted to get back to where he belonged. *Back to Earth. Maybe this isn't so much fun after all. I don't like having guns pointed at me.*

"Do you really want to anger Dracanna by holding her people?" Sassy asked. "Her treats may be sweet, but she is widely known for her sour disposition. When her icy exterior melts, the fire beneath has destroyed worlds."

"We're safe here on Mongoleon," the Insectoid holding the man snapped. "She wouldn't dare anger the Kahn." He spit a glob of blue goo onto the floor.

"And if she should get the Kahn's forces to help her in her search for these two, then what?" Sassy pulled Conrad and Travis closer to his shaggy sides.

"When was the last time the Kahn cared about anything other than his own wants and desires?"

"There's always a first time," Sassy replied. His hand released Conrad and disappeared into the shaggy fur at his hip.

"What's going on?" Travis muttered, sounding more coherent than he had moments before.

The Insectoid with the gun swung his attention toward him. Sassy's hand jerked out of his fur holding an unbelievably big gun.

"Now, I suggest you let me take the Earthlings back to Dracanna and prevent a complication that we really do not need right now!" Sassy roared as he trained the weapon on the gun-toting insect.

The tensions in the room climbed. Conrad felt sure that if the insect people could sweat, they were. His blouse was soaked through. He didn't have a weapon. He didn't see anything he could do to improve the situation. His only hope was that the Insectoids would see Sassy as a bigger threat than their own guy with the gun and not blast them to smithereens.

Sassy glared at the insect through brow-shaded dark-brown eyes.

The insect glared back through multi-faceted eyes that moments before glittered with many different colors, but now just reflected Sassy's shaggy-brown form.

The tension rose.

Fingers twitched.

Sassy's brow ridge furrowed.

If the insect had brows they would have followed suit.

With the strangeness of the situation, Conrad expected cheesy spaghetti western music to start up as the two faced off.

"Where is my next subject?" a high ethereal voice demanded.

Conrad looked away from the two gun toters. A chill went through him. The urge to run back into the cocoon and hide washed over him. Here was something that walked out of the fears of nearly every human from prehistoric to modern man.

A Gray walked into the room.

***

"Come on sweetie, you've got to come up with a better answer than that," Bea Mann said.

"That's all I can figure," Scoop replied. "I've been trying every possible scan Shoppe and I can do. They are either somewhere that is heavily shielded or they're off planet. Trust me, Shoppe is frantic over Conrad."

Bea sighed and clicked her shiny red nails on the glass freezer top. "What's with Shoppe and Conrad anyway? Did she catch him in the bathroom beating off and liked what she saw, or something?"

Scoop paused before answering, then let out an odd noise which could only be a sigh since the implement didn't have the lungs needed to make a normal sigh. "I don't know. When I ask her about it, she gets all quiet, but there's definitely something about that man that has caught her attention. She's not acted like this toward anyone since Dracanna first came on board."

"I didn't realize you'd been with the two of them that long." Bea stopped her drumming to scrutinize Scoop.

"I've been around a lot longer than I like to think about," Scoop replied. "But right now, we need to try to figure out how to find Conrad and Travis. You know, there might be something useful in the Darkholmian ship. If his tech is newer, we might be able to use it to penetrate whatever's shielding the guys."

"You know I'm all about penetration, but do you know enough about their tech to use it?" Bea asked. If they hadn't been in the middle of a crisis, she would've been a little upset about the change of subject. *I'll have to see what*

106

I can do about getting the info out of Scoop later.

"I think Shoppe can get us past the door locks, so if she can get us in, I can get us into the computer system." Scoop fell silent. "She thinks she can get us in. Do you mind carrying me back to the dressing room?"

"Sure, but I thought Dracanna just had Shoppe updated." Bea replied, picking up Scoop.

"There's a vast difference between current Darkholmian tech and the aftermarket stuff Dracanna can get her painted nails on. Let's just say, Shoppe got upgraded to a Delorian and this other ship is the equivalent to a Tesla."

They reached the dressing room, which was still in a state of disarray, even though Dracanna had moved Rice's body off to the freezers until they could get back to Earth and return it to her family. Wardrobe lay scattered about. A couple of piles were bigger than others, where they'd moved things around, while getting ready for the Kahn's dinner. On the far wall, the outline of a door that Bea had never seen before beckoned ominously.

"Shoppe says that we can go on in. There isn't an AI active on the ship," Scoop said as Bea maneuvered through the mess. "That's very strange. Most newer Darkholmians rely almost exclusively on their AIs to pilot their ships. I wonder why Wren disabled his."

"Who knows, and I really don't care at this point." Bea squared her broad shoulders. "Let's just get through that door and see what we can find on the other side. Hopefully their scanners are better than ours." The door opened as she approached. She didn't say anything, but she hoped it was Shoppe opening the way for them. She wasn't in the mood to be dealing with spooky ghost ships. Beyond the door, darkness awaited them.

***

Conrad gulped as he stared at the Gray standing in the doorway. The creature was much taller than the little one Genghis Kahn had in the cage at dinner. It was nearly human sized, complete with broad shoulders and a cleft chin. Like the other one, there was no evidence of sex, but there was something about this one that screamed masculine. He knew a few dykes that pulled that off well, so it didn't really help him figure anything out.

"Sasalmater, please tell me that you're not trying to help these humans to escape," the asexual-voiced creature asked. Its huge dark eyes focused on the Sasquatch. Conrad was glad it had turned from him.

"Hey, these two don't know anything about Genghis and his plans," the big creature replied. He squared his shoulders but didn't lower his gun from the Insectoid it was still trained on. "Not only that, but they are new employees of Dracanna's. Do you really think it's a good idea to upset Dracanna?"

"Hey, I'm not an employee," Travis said. "Conrad's the one in the skirt." He sounded stronger by the minute and that made Conrad feel better about their chances of getting out of the mess they were in.

"Dracanna is a well-known friend of the Kahn," the Gray said, apparently ignoring Travis' outburst. "It is unknown if she will back him or remain neutral in our conflict with the tyrant." The black eyes stared at Conrad, and he wanted to crawl behind Sassy's shaggy bulk to escape the gaze. "What can you tell me?" As the question left the thing's miniscule mouth, something tugged at Conrad's brain. He lost his fear and only wanted to obey.

"I don't know anything about what she has planned. Until earlier today, I thought she just ran an ice cream shop.

I didn't even know I was going to have to wear a dress to work there."

The Gray laughed. It was a mirthless sound that chilled Conrad in a way that the ice cream freezers never could. "You silly humans think so much of your clothes. You seek to hide your sexuality by choosing the clothes of whatever gender you believe you are identifying with at the time. As you evolve, should your species live that long, you will discover that there is more to sexuality than the clothes you wear and how you act. Why do you think the more evolved races in the galaxy have done away with any such trappings? Do you see anyone here, other than humans, who requires clothes and attitudes to define them?"

Conrad didn't know what to say. He had no idea how to identify males from females in any of the three species he was now facing. *The Insectoids are just large bugs as far as I can tell. I don't even know how to tell male from female bugs back in Texas. The Gray is just an asexual alien and Sassy is...well Sassy.* He only knew Sassy was male from the conversation the bigfoot had with Bea back when the shop was still on Earth.

He shrugged. "I guess not."

"Of course not. Clothing and the whole idea that it defines one's sexuality is a totally human concept, and a backward one at that. No matter what you are wearing, I could tell that you are the male of the species. Your genitalia is much too pronounced to be female."

"Hey, my genitalia is not pronounced," Conrad objected, his hands reflexively covering his crotch. *How does he know my genitalia is pronounced?*

"It is more pronounced than the one who wears male clothing." The Gray's dark eyes moved from Conrad to Travis.

"Hey, it's more than a little cold in here," Travis complained with a blush.

"So, how do you tell your males from your females?" Conrad asked, embarrassment emboldening him. *Travis is nice, it doesn't matter if he's hung or not.*

The Gray smiled. "That is one of the secrets of my race. It is something that only we know." It turned its attention back to Sassy and the Insectoid. "Now if you two would kindly put away your guns, and return your respective prisoners to their cocoons and pull out a wife for me, we can proceed with the interrogations. We need to know what the Kahn is planning so we can plot accordingly. Time is running out if we are to rescue Meridia Twelve and free this quadrant from his iron fist."

"Who is Meridia Twelve?" Conrad asked before he could stop himself. *Maybe if I can keep the alien talking, it'll give Sassy time to think up a way out for all of us.*

The Gray's gaze bore into him. It sent shivers through Conrad's mind. The smooth pale skin of the creature's forehead creased.

"Meridia Twelve, is the twelfth of her name. She is not a warrior, and truth be told, not much of a lover, but she was my lover. She had a meticulous mind when it came to science. Two thousand of your years ago, she was the pilot of a ship that had been sent to study your species. She was careless and was captured by Genghis Kahn. For all these years, I've been searching for a way to get her back, and right the terrible wrong that has been wrought on the universe."

Conrad gulped. *I've seen Meridia Twelve. She'd been in a cage during dinner. She looked so sad and pathetic.* His heart broke thinking of her.

"We can help you," he proclaimed.

Sassy and Travis both stared at him. Disbelief was clearly written on their very different faces.

5
Apple Pie Alamode

Dracanna glared at the guard who barred her from the Kahn's chambers. She had stood there patiently in the opulent hall for over ten minutes waiting for something to happen. A page had been dispatched but so far had not returned. The guard pulled his heavy fox-trimmed hat lower over his eyes as if to avoid her stare. Finally the page returned and led her into the formal audience chamber.

"Ah Dracanna, have you succeeded where my men have failed?" Genghis asked as she approached his throne. The large chair was not as lavish as most thrones. It was more of a camp chair. Above it was a billowing tapestry of Genghis in the Gray ship as he descended on the desert planet he dubbed Mongoleon.

She stopped a couple of steps from the chair. The cage on the left was empty. *Where is Gyre?*

"Sadly, no." She gazed into the face that so few people hazarded to look upon. No sign of age dared show there, but now that she really looked at it, the tired lines were obvious. Bags shadowed his eyes. His moustache drooped a little further than normal. This made her wonder how long the Insectoids and Grays had been working together against him. "I have Bea and Rice working on the problem."

"Ah, so the lovely Rice is feeling better," he said. "I must stop by and see her soon, or perhaps you could send her to me."

Dracanna shook her head. "She's still very under the weather, but I found things she could do. Shoppe's sensors can't locate my missing crew. I suspect they are in a shielded place, or off planet."

"Not possible!" The Kahn slammed his fist down on the sturdy wooden arms of his chair. "My men report no unauthorized ships either near the planet or having left the surface since before the attack during dinner. They are still searching the city and surrounding desert for the missing. They took people we need back!"

Dracanna wanted to argue that anyone who had been stolen at any time was worthy of getting back, but she didn't feel like debating the value of life with the galactic dictator. She had more important things to do with her time.

"I actually came here on an equally important matter. I need to get some repairs done to Shoppe. As I previously mentioned, our arrival was not as smooth as normal, and I need to get some replacement tables made. The merchant I normally deal with tells me some of the ingredients needed to make the tables have been placed on a restricted list by your government."

The Kahn leaned back in his chair and looked down at her. A new, hungry expression crossed his face. There was something he wanted out of her.

"My men have been trying to duplicate the way your ship travels." A previously unheard note of caution entered his voice. "There is something special about it. I restricted access to the items that you purchased here on Mongoleon in the past so that perhaps you would share some of your secrets with me the next time you were in need of assistance, or maintenance."

Dracanna had suspected as much. *Genghis has had his beady little brown eyes on Shoppe since I first met him. He's crafty. He'd never try to outright take the ship from me, but he'd try to get whatever information he could to duplicate things. He'd learned that trick from Gyre. The Grays are masters at study and replication of everything they come in contact with from technology to genes, although sometimes I suspect they do their anal probing for more than just scientific curiosity.*

"Genghis, you know Darkholmian technology is more complex than even the Grays can figure out. Hell, we don't even know how most of it works. It's a combination of science, and magic with a healthy dose of luck thrown in for good measure."

"That *is* what my ambassador to your father's court tells me," the Kahn replied. "He also tells me that your father is working with several other races to make advancements to that technology. There are rumors that he may at long last be sharing things with other races."

Dracanna's head spun. *Wren said my father is gravely ill. Does that tie into his sharing sacred technology with others? Has he made some kind of deal that invalidated the deals that give the royal house of Darkholme our ability to travel so effortlessly about?* She didn't have time to think about that. She had to get Shoppe repaired and find her missing crewmembers.

"What do you want?" she sighed. She knew she was craftier than the Kahn; it came with being who and what she was. She could give him just enough to get him to give her what she needed, but not enough to give him a new means to conquer more of the galaxy.

Genghis smiled and his drooping mustache rose. "Show my shamans how to cast the spell to call the spirit of the vessels."

Dracanna wondered how far the Mongolians had progressed in their research if that was what he wanted. It was one of the trickier parts of the ship creation—a part Darkholmians had been trying to remove to use more reliable AIs instead. In truth, there wasn't a whole lot of difference between an AI and a summoned spirit. But she wouldn't trade Shoppe and her feistiness for any computer board in the entire universe.

"I'll have to see if your shamans are capable of casting the spells."

He laughed. "You'll find them extremely capable, or they wouldn't still be alive."

A chill went through Dracanna. *Somehow, I don't doubt that for an instant.*

***

"We can what?" Travis stared at Conrad, disbelief etched on his handsome face.

"We can help them," Conrad repeated. His mind whirled as he tried to think of ways they could help in the fight against the Kahn. He'd seen the little Gray in the cage. It'd touched something in him. Something at the core of his being screamed it was wrong. *It's worse than seeing a bored gorilla in a zoo. This is an intelligent creature held captive by a man who had conquered a large chunk of Earth before his empire fell.* Now he knew it fell because Genghis Kahn had left Earth to begin his conquest of the galaxy. He didn't know if they could stop his tyrannical rule, but they could at least free one little Gray.

115

"Conrad, do you know what you're saying?" Sassy asked, finally lowering his gun from the Insectoid. "If you make a deal with Thorial Five and you fail, you and Travis will be his. The odds are he'll incorporate some of your DNA into his own, making you a part of him."

"Look, I may be an average gay man from Dallas, Texas who hasn't worked since he got out of the Air Force, but I have my limits. I don't like to see people, animals, or aliens abused. Okay. So she made a mistake and unleashed a tyrant who has taken over a quarter of the galaxy, but she's still alive and deserves our help. I'll do what I can, even in this damnable skirt!" He paused and dropped his voice. "And if I fail…well Thorial there looks like he could use a little enhancement, if you know what I mean."

Sassy choked back a laugh. It sounded a bit like a hairball.

Travis came around to the other side of the Sasquatch and touched Conrad's arm. "Do you get this butch all the time?"

Heat rose in Conrad's cheeks. "Not all the time."

"It's kinda cute."

"So you will help us?" Thorial asked. If he'd had a nose, he would've been looking down it at Conrad.

"Yeah, we'll do what we can," Conrad replied. "We need to get back to the Scary Queen and see if Dracanna knows of anything we can do to help."

Thorial shook his bald head. "I'm sorry, we are unsure of where the dark lady's loyalties lie. She has been a longtime supporter of the Kahn."

"Then do you have an idea?" he asked. Travis's hand slipped into his. The large fingers squeezed supportively. His warmth lent Conrad strength.

"We have been trying to find a weakness in the

Kahn's residence," the Gray said. "Unfortunately, since we have been stepping up the rebellion, he's increased his protections. The special dinner he threw last night for the arrival of your employer was at one of the special occasion yurts that he hasn't gotten around to fortifying yet. That allowed our Insectoid allies to dig in and get you out. Right after the attack, he retreated to his bunker that's made of reinforced metalicrete that the Insectoids cannot burrow into. The entire planet is protected by his space armada, so it's been fifteen hundred years since any Gray ship has been able to get close enough to get troops easily on or off the surface. There are fewer ships in orbit than normal, but we are not sure why that is."

"So how did you get here?" Conrad asked. "And I thought I saw some of your kind in the market yesterday." While they talked, the two Insectoids returned the Mongol captive to his cocoon. At least the guns had all been lowered.

"Sometimes, some of our allies, like Sasalmater, will use their special talents to get us into places we need to be. What you saw in the market place were most likely one of the many lesser races that resemble us. No real Gray has legally been here, and wouldn't be out in public where it could be spotted."

Conrad turned to the Sasquatch. "So Sassy, what can you do to help out here?"

The huge creature's shoulders heaved. "The main compound is protected from my ability to move from one place to another. His shamans have seen to that. Otherwise, I or one of the others, would've already gotten her back. We don't know for sure, but we suspect they had the magical protections set up before he left Earth."

"Wait a minute…there's magic too?" Conrad wished

117

there was a place he could sit down. A bit more info poured into his mind that he wanted to deal with. *Had the ice cream demon been magical?*

"There are fine lines between magic and science," Thorial said. "I believe one of your own race said at times there is no difference between advanced science and magic. For many of your millennia, our race has been seen as everything from gods, to fairies and even today, you are not sure if we are advanced life forms, or magical creatures. A vast amount of our power comes from our brains. This allows us to channel our thoughts and impact the universe around us. It was through his shamans that Genghis managed to master our technology so quickly. They adapted our mental tech to their magical minds; it took us completely by surprise."

"Your tech all runs by you thinking at it?" Travis asked.

"Crudely put, but yes."

"Then why haven't you just thought your significant other out of the cage?" the cowboy continued.

"There is something about the Mongolians that makes them immune to us. Their shamans block our efforts at affecting the world around them. One of the reasons that Meridia Twelve was studying the Mongols was to find out what it is that makes them immune. I continue her work even to this day, and haven't been able to determine the exact gene sequence that causes the strange mutation. If anything, the mutation has grown stronger since they came into space."

Conrad wasn't sure how much more he could handle. The details the Gray spilled out were nearly useless. "Okay, so do you have any plan on how to proceed?"

"We have been trying to find some sympathizers in

the Kahn's people who might be able to get past the guards and smuggle Meridia Twelve out," Thorial replied. "Unfortunately, even though he represses his own people, they are not willing to rise up against him."

"You've been using hit and run tactics to get his attention," Conrad replied. He'd seen the tactic before, when he'd been in the Middle East. It caused chaos, but wasn't effective in the long term.

"Yes, unfortunately, we haven't been able to cause enough of an uproar to get more than a few guards at a time drawn away."

"How many troops do we have at our disposal?" Conrad asked. "How big of a disturbance can we create?"

"Our largest group is the Insectoids," Sassy took over the narrative. "This was their planet before the Kahn took it over, feeling it was most like the desert he so loved back on Earth. His troops relentlessly slaughtered them until only a few hidden hives remain. They are fighting because their latest queen has decided they need to take back their planet. There are a handful of Grays. They are mostly acting as advisors. I can get a large number of Sasquatches and Yetis here if we need them. Might even be able to bring in more Grays as we come."

Conrad fingered some of the golden fringe along the waistband of his skirt. "So what is the ultimate goal, just to rescue Meridia Twelve, or completely overthrow Genghis Kahn?"

"The Kahn," one of the Insectoids spat another glob of blue goo, "must go. Our queen demands it!"

Thorial nodded in agreement. "For too long he has terrorized space. The citizens of the galaxy, no, the universe, will thank us for disposing of him."

Remembering the chaos of removing leaders with no

plan on who would fill their shoes, Conrad scratched his head. *Who steps in to take control of the empire?*

***

Bea and Scoop entered the darkened hall of the Darkholmian ship. Soft lights came up. Barely pushing the shadows away, they just added to the already creepy vibe. Bea had to remember that Dracanna's people were vampires of a sort. They liked dark places.

"So how do we find the control room, bridge or whatever this thing has?" she asked.

"Shoppe says she's going to illuminate the path for us," Scoop replied. "It's been a while since I was in a Darkholmian ship and not a newer model like this. This thing is so modern…it's soulless."

Bea shivered and clutched Scoop tightly in her strong, freckled hand. "Dracanna never took me to Darkholme. I always thought she was trying to avoid the place. I can see why."

"You have no idea. For years she's stayed ahead of them, moving from planet to planet. Having Shoppe appear as an epicurean establishment is a great cover. It also helps keep money coming in."

"But ice cream's only been around so long." Bea said as they turned a corner.

"True," Scoop agreed. "But before that, there were candy stores, and opium dens—so many ways for us to stay hidden on your world and many others. Something in my metal tells me that Wren finding us now is not a coincidence, something big is about to happen."

A door swooshed open, and they stepped into a small room full of panels with a central chair positioned to control them all.

"Take the seat," Scoop suggested.

120

"Is it safe?" Bea bent a bit to get her tall frame into the cramped area.

"Shoppe still hasn't been able to establish communications with the AI. I'm concerned something may be wrong, but sitting in the chair shouldn't be a problem while we attempt to access the ship's computer system."

Bea settled into the soft cushioned seat. As she relaxed into it, straps and clamps sprang out, encircling her.

"Scoop, do something!" she screamed. She struggled, but was held tight to the chair.

***

Dracanna ignored the guards that flanked the door she strolled through. She'd never been this deep into Genghis' stronghold before. The primitive, traditional Mongolian world of rough hide walls and ornate rugs gave way to a sleek metal corridor, a more high tech existence that reminded the proprietress of the Scary Queen more of a Gray world. *I've been on their spaceships, so I really shouldn't be overly surprised, but on the home world, this is amazing. Genghis likes to keep his home pure.*

Then, abruptly as it began, the high tech ended and the trappings of Mongolian life reappeared as she walked into the next, unguarded room.

"So the Khan thinks *you* can teach *us* some magic," a stocky man said as the door closed behind Dracanna. He was short, even by Mongolian standards. His flabby shoulders were covered in a variety of skins, most from creatures she didn't recognize.

But then I'm not the safari type. "That's what he seems to think." Her gaze passed over the other seven people in the room. More Mongolians, all but one, clothed similarly to the stocky sarcastic man.

"And what are your qualifications to teach magic to

us?" Mister Sarcastic continued.

"I'm older than any of you and have seen more of this universe and the planes that run parallel to it than you could even begin to comprehend," Dracanna snapped. "I know more of science and magic than nearly any other being alive today." She didn't bother to add that, on the whole, Darkholmians were one of the most advanced races in the known universe. They should already know that.

"Prove it!" Sarcastic shouted. "Control the spirit in the bowl in front of you before it gets loose."

Dracanna spotted the altar in the center of the room with a rough, unfinished wooden bowl sitting on its alabaster top. An odd, sulfur-smelling smoke rose scarlet from the bowl. A Cathode demon. *It's a strange thing for them to call up so near the high tech of Genghis' central command. If it manages to escape the shamans, it could cause incredible damage to the equipment that would draw it like a bear to honey. Are they really that careless, or is this a clever way of saying they know more tech than they appear to?* She raised one well-groomed black eyebrow as the possibilities for this little creature came into her head. *But first I have to get it under my control.*

"What a quaint little thing it is." Dracanna smiled as she walked toward the altar. She dug into the bottomless clutch purse she carried, fishing out a small vial and an oriental fan. With a flick of her wrist, she opened the fan as she approached the demon.

Around her, the shamans drew in a breath, a dangerous thing to do in the presence of a gas-based demon. When it managed to possess humans or other physical beings, a Cathode demon was normally inhaled and took up residence in the lungs. The species really enjoyed getting into cyborgs. Luckily, there weren't many of those around the Mongolian sector. It was rumored they gave Genghis the creeps.

Uncapping the vial, Dracanna gave the fan an initial swish. The scarlet smoke rose steadily into the air, seemingly unaffected by the fan, but it let out a high-pitched wail that caused the gathered shamans to cover their ears.

"None of that, my pretty," Dracanna said. She smiled as the words to a nasty binding spell came into her mind. She held the vial up and swished the fan vigorously to blow the smoke toward the open glass mouth.

"When wisps of smoke I do find, thoughts of demons come to mind. When smoky demons I do find, these I know that I must bind. In this vial now you'll find a binding straight and true." The scarlet smoke continued to wail as it flowed from the bowl to the vial. "Here you bide until the spell I undo. And at that time you'll do, whatever I have in mind." A little tinkle sounded as the tiny solid fragment of the Cathode demon landed in the vial and the final wisp of smoke circled around the top before vanishing like piss down a toilet. Dracanna smiled as she secured the plastic top to the vial before lifting it to peer at the swirling scarlet smoke inside. A tiny face glared back at her. She laughed as she returned the vial and the fan to her black clutch.

"Anything tougher you'd like me to do?" she asked. *I wish ice cream demons were as easy to deal with as Cathodes. Then we wouldn't be in this mess.* Even the sarcastic one was a little cowed, but not so much that he didn't still have a few questions for her—questions that she artfully answered in an effort to get what she needed without giving away too much information

***

"Alright, we need a good plan," Conrad said. "Other than grabbing us during the dinner, have any of your plans actually worked out?"

"We are good at causing chaos," an Insectoid chirped. So far, Conrad hadn't been able to figure out how to tell one bug from another. They all looked alike unless they were carrying something or wearing something. After they all decided to work together, the guns disappeared, leaving him clueless to each one's identity.

"Chaos will only get you so far. You need a good plan," he continued. "What are the Kahn's forces like?"

"He controls the surface of the planet with a combination of ground troops and orbiting spaceships," Sassy said before any of the aliens could. "Using the captured Gray tech, he can get a large number of troops anywhere on the planet in a few minutes."

"How so?" Travis asked.

"It's like that one freezer in the Scary Queen," the Sasquatch said.

Conrad's brows came together in confusion. "Which freezer?"

"I think you and Bea were filling it when I came in and met you for the first time. When the shop isn't somewhere on Earth that we can access it; one of the freezers acts as a dimensional doorway, allowing those of us who can walk across dimensional boundaries to get to you. Some of us can't go too long without our ice cream."

"So Genghis has a technology that allows his troops to move across dimensional borders?" Conrad asked. "That's cool."

"Well, they act more like doorways. They go from one point to another, but they open both ways. I don't know if they can open to multiple locations, or a fixed terminus." Sassy scratched his head and pulled out a pine needle which he just dropped casually on the floor.

"They are based on our tech, and it is a fixed terminus," Thorial Five added. "We never mastered being able to move points on our gateways, so each gate only opens to one place."

"That's good," Conrad said. "That gives us hope to block the gateways if we can take out the central location where they all originate. They do open onto a central location, don't they?"

Thorial shook his hairless head. "No, they have several hubs across the planet where the ships open gateways to. They also have gateways between the individual ships to make it easier to move troops around up there."

"Is there any kind of central hub for the ship? Anything that could make it difficult for them to move people around? Can these things be jammed or interrupted in any way?"

"There is a point where there is a high orbit station just beyond the fifth moon---" one of the Insectoids began.

"Wait," Conrad cut him off. "This planet has five moons?" *From the little that I know about moons that would make for very chaotic weather patterns.*

"That's one of the reasons it's a desert world," Sassy explained. "The gravity from so many moons makes it hard to sustain surface water."

Conrad held up his hand. "Sorry for interrupting, it didn't help with the planning. I just haven't ever been on a planet with more than one moon before."

Sassy laughed and patted his shoulder like he was some kind of cute kid. "It's okay, Conrad. We all understand the wonders of new worlds around here."

"So, back to this hub out by the fifth moon, if we can disrupt it, will it help us stop more troops from getting down here when we storm the yurt to rescue Meridia Twelve?"

"It would slow them down." Thorial said. "Unfortunately it isn't possible to disrupt the whole gate gridwork."

"Wait a minute," Conrad smacked his head. "If their gateways are built on your tech, can't you guys just hack into them?"

"No," the Gray replied. "They have corrupted our tech with their magic. Their gateways only work for those of Mongolian ancestry."

"Alright, so how do we get up to their hub to slow them down?" Travis asked, drawing Conrad closer to him. Concern radiated out from him. In other situations it might have been a little clingy, but there was something about having Travis at his side that made things feel better.

"My people might be able to help with that." Sassy leaned against a nearby wall. "Most of their off-world stuff isn't shielded as heavily as the planet-bound locations. But for it to be effective, we're going to need to do it at the same time as folks here are attacking Genghis' place to make the most of our effort. But we still don't know how we're going to get folks into the yurt. Since the latest attack, the odds are if any of us nonhumans so much as show our faces on the streets of Genghis, we'll be shot on sight. The guards are constantly updated as to which species are legal and which aren't. Even though it changes from time to time, depending on who's on the outs with the Khan, Gray's have been outlawed for longer than a lot a species can remember."

Conrad smiled and smoothed a wrinkle out of his skirt. "I think I have an idea on that. But it means we have to trust Dracanna."

***

"Bea, be calm," Scoop shouted above the Bea's

hysterics.

"*You* be calm," she snapped. "You're not the one strapped into a chair in the middle of an alien spacecraft." Sweat ran down her back and coated her palms. She didn't want to think about what it was doing to her makeup.

"Actually, since you're holding onto me right now, I'm as immobilized as you."

Bea took a deep breath and tried to calm her automatic panic response. *Scoop's right, getting hysterical isn't going to help either of us.* She tried to muscle her way out of the straps. They'd clamped down tighter than a Madonna cone bra.

"So what are we going to do?"

"Give me a minute to chat with Shoppe," Scoop replied. "See if she has any ideas on how to get us out of here. I'm still worried that the AI isn't functioning."

"Well if the AI isn't working then what the hell is making this chair hold on to me worse than a clinging boytoy?" Bea sighed and tried desperately to relax. *Get ahold of yourself, Bitch, you've been in tighter spots than this. If nothing else, Dracanna will come back, notice us missing and come looking for us.*

"I don't know," Scoop snapped. The metal of his handle grew cold in her large warm hand.

The Darkholmian ship shook, throwing Bea against the metal bands restraining her.

"Now what?"

"Shoppe lost contact with Dracanna," Scoop replied. "She tried to take off again and can't get anywhere. She's getting very upset."

"Look, I understand upset!" Bea screamed. Her attempt at calm went flying out the proverbial window. "I hope she can hear me, because right now, this flighty spaceship needs to pull her shit together and act like a grownup as opposed to a little bitch who isn't getting her way!" She took another deep calming breath. "We all have to stay calm and figure out how to get through the next little while. I'm sure her Bitchiness is just fine. She probably entered into some heavily shielded room or something."

"Shoppe says, thank you, Miss Bea," Scoop replied evenly, his metal handle warming a bit. "It has been a hard day on all of us."

Bea nodded as much as the metal restraint around her neck would allow. "I understand. So lots of deep breaths, even for those of us who don't breathe, and let's figure out how to get me out of these straps and find our friends. If there's one thing I don't need, it's strap-ons." *When Dracanna gets back, she's getting an earful about the things that she does to stress out Shoppe and what it does to the rest of us when things go haywire around here. If I'm still able to talk by then.*

***

"Now, the complicated part of the spell is trying to find an appropriate spirit to pilot a vessel," Dracanna explained to the shamans gathered around her. "You can't just pull any old spirit out of the ether to pilot a space ship. It's harder than finding a good driver in Houston, Texas."

"And where do you look for proper spirits?" asked the sarcastic shaman, whose name was actually Axel.

"Bird spirits are usually good, as are former race car drivers," Dracanna said, from her seat on several cushions spread out around the altar. "Now do any of you know any former race car drivers?"

They all shook their heads. "What are race car drivers?" asked the one wearing no animal skins.

"Oh my." Dracanna gasped in mock surprise. "I'd

forgotten that none of you know what race cars are." She thought for a moment. "How about jockeys? Although it doesn't require as much in the way of piloting skills, jockeys do have to steer horses and hang on." *Not at all traits you want in a sentient spaceship, but who knows, if Genghis gets a bunch of adrenalin junky spaceships he might lose most of them the first couple of months out of the chute. Nothing like the thrill of doing a slingshot maneuver around a sun to get a ship fried.*

"We have a number of failed horse racers," Axel said. "It is not an honorable death when one of the Kahn's men fail him at the races. You think their spirits would be good to inhabit living space ships?"

Dracanna pinched the bridge of her nose and shook her ebony-locked head. "No, not the losers, you need winners. They are the ones that have the control needed to navigate a ship through the stars."

"I know of one," No-Skins said. "My fifth wife's brother was a very popular and successful horse racer before his steed stumbled during a race and the two of them tumbled off a cliff into the river."

Perfect, Dracanna nodded, *this guy was so competent he managed to ride a horse right into the only river on a desert planet.* "He would be great for this. So how many spaceships do you have ready for spirits to drive them?"

"Four hundred," Axel replied. Dracanna's heart stopped. Genghis had already managed to get four hundred ships built and was waiting for spirits to inhabit them. *Will any of time and space be safe from the tyrant and his plans? But then if I can manage to get idiot spirits to drive them all, I have hope. I never figured the weight of the universe would rest on my narrow shoulders. Maybe I can keep these guys bumbling around long enough for the uprising to occur.*

***

"Your plan may be sound, Conrad," Thorial said. "I'm still not sure we can trust Dracanna not to betray us to Genghis Kahn, but it is worth pursuing."

"I'll go round up some of my people," Sassy said. "Be back in a little while. Don't do anything without me." The big Sasquatch stepped back into the shadows and disappeared.

"I shall contact Gray High Command to see if they can spare any warriors or ships." Thorial turned and walked out of the cocoon room, leaving Conrad and Travis with the two Insectoids.

"We shall inform our queen of the situation," one of them clicked. "If you could please wait here." Then they scuttled off.

"Well this certainly wasn't how I planned on my day going." Travis eased himself down onto the hard metal floor.

Conrad chuckled as he settled in next to the handsome cowboy. "I know. I figured I'd be home by now, out of the dress and makeup." He glanced at his watch. "Well hell, I'd actually be more than half way through my next day at work by now. I guess we're never sure how life is going to turn out, are we?" He yawned. *The time in the cocoon wasn't much in the way of sleep, but I've got to hold it together a while longer.*

Travis smiled at him. It was a warm inviting smile and made his heart beat a little faster. "Life not going as you planned normally involves a water pipe bursting when you're trying to get ready for a date, or accidentally picking up decaf as opposed to premium roast, not getting attacked by an ice cream monster, being hurled through time and space, almost stampeded by a herd of Mongolian ponies, then being kidnapped by insect aliens and finally trying to overthrow Genghis Kahn. This goes a little bit beyond 'not as planned'." He tilted his handsome head and looked at Conrad through his piercing blue eyes. "But hey, I'm getting to know you better." He reached out and caught Conrad's hand. "You're a nice guy, Conrad Bale, even if they do call you Cat Astrophe, and you like to wear dresses."

Conrad frowned. "I don't *like* to wear dresses. Do you think those guys at clown town like to wear the silly little uniforms? That's all this is, a silly little uniform for those of us who get jobs with the Scary Queen. But thanks, you're a nice guy too, Travis Sinclair."

"So, when we get back to Earth, would you mind going out on a date, something quiet, maybe dinner and a movie?" Travis asked. "You wouldn't have to wear the skirt. You look great in jeans."

"Thanks." Conrad's face split into a huge grin. Even here in the strange metal room, surrounded by Mongolians encased in alien cocoons, it felt good to have Travis asking him out. "I hope we survive long enough to enjoy ourselves."

Travis leaned over and kissed Conrad. His lips were warm and inviting. Conrad's heart pounded.

Something scratched behind them. The two men jerked apart, and Conrad turned to see Thorial leaning against the doorway.

"Oh don't mind me. Please continue your courting ritual," the Gray said. "I find the study of other species and their intimate habits most entertaining."

"We're supposed to be planning a revolution here," Conrad replied, struggling to his feet. "We were just taking a few minutes talking."

"The last time I checked, your species requires air passing through your vocal cords to speak," Thorial replied.

"There have been a few members that have exhibited a certain level of telepathy, but I doubt either of you has mastered that talent. But in primitive cases, it can be amplified by touch."

"Look, don't worry about what we were just doing." Conrad tried to sound calm even though he wanted to punch the alien for interrupting the first real romantic moment he'd been able to share with Travis. "What did your high command have to say?"

The Gray nodded, but the odd twist to his narrow mouth still looked like a smile to Conrad. "They are waiting for Sasalmater and his people to arrive and provide transport for our ground troops. Our ships are making toward the star gates as we speak and will be arriving in Mongoleon space in the next two hours."

"Our Queen is rallying the other hives." A lone Insectoid came into the room. "We will be ready in hours as well."

"All we need now is a bit of apple pie and some ice cream, and we'll be ready for a revolutionary celebration." Travis grinned and his blue eyes sparkled at Conrad.

He wondered *Is Travis getting turned on by all the war talk, or did he feel the fireworks in our kiss? I hope it was our kiss. It was a really great kiss. I just hope it isn't our, or even my, last kiss.*

***

Inwardly, Bea sighed. She wasn't sure how long she'd been strapped to the command chair in the strange Darkholmian ship, but she was over it. Shoppe had been trying to reactivate the AI that controlled the ship to no avail. Wren had done an excellent job sabotaging it. The ship was cold, and Bea had a crick in her neck.

"This really makes no sense at all," Scoop said again.

"Especially if there is no spirit controlling the ship, there should be an AI. They encountered us when we were traveling through time and space. No one that I've ever heard of can manually pilot a craft through time. The navigation is just too difficult."

"Well, maybe he's just some kind of super genius that can do everything without help," Bea snapped. Her temper was growing short at her confinement.

"I've met him before, or actually I've met people from his house before," Scoop said. "They're all a bunch of snot-nosed sycophants. Not really much better than basic political monkeys and errand boys for the ruling house. I wonder if he has some kind of cybernetic implant or something that allows him to control the ship. Maybe that's it. The AI is still on him somewhere." The implement became silent.

"What's wrong Scoop?" The sudden quiet disturbed her.

"Checking with Shoppe to see if she can detect the AI in the freezer where we've got Wren on ice."

"And?"

"She's not getting anything. If it's there, hopefully the intense cold has the computer shut down as well as the vampire, but it gives me an idea." He went silent again. It was one of the things that Bea hated about Scoop. There was really no way to tell if the consciousness that inhabited the kitchen utensil was really there, or off talking to Shoppe, which he did quite a lot.

"Bea, can you move me far enough down that I can touch the chair?" he asked, suddenly back from talking with Shoppe.

"If I can bend my wrist far enough. The arms of this chair were designed for someone with much shorter arms than I have." Careful not to drop the ice cream scoop, Bea slid the handle through her large fingers until she just held onto the bowl at the top, then she bent her wrist so the end of the handle touched the metal arm of the chair. A small jolt of power leapt from Scoop to the chair. It tingled along Bea's arm. She nearly jerked back, but forced herself to hold steady.

"Ah, I'd hoped so," Scoop said. "I think I can access the computer as if I were the AI. It may take a minute or two for me to find the right circuits to force it to let you go."

"Take your time, it's not like I'm at normal angles here or anything." Bea held onto the tip of Scoop while the haunted hand tool tried to communicate with the ship. Her wrist began to ache from the odd angle she needed to hold it to keep him touching the chair.

"There we go," Scoop said, "I think I found the circuit to release the bands on the chair."

The bands suddenly tightened around Bea. "Nope!" she gasped as the band around her throat constricted. She jerked and the metal bit into her harder. The edges of the bands dug in to the point that her wrists bled slightly.

"Oops!" Scoop replied. "Let's try the other way." And the bands clicked open and slid back into their hiding places around the chair. Bea scrambled out of the seat.

"Set me back against the arm," Scoop said as Bea rubbed her neck with her unencumbered hand. "Maybe I can get this thing working enough we can use its sensor array."

Bea placed him down so he touched the metal. "As long as I don't have to sit back down in it, you can go wherever you damn well please."

"This may take a few minutes."

"I'm out of the damned chair," Bea snarled, rubbing her wrists. "Take all the time you need." *Luckily, I'm not bleeding too much. I'll find some bandages in a few minutes when we get back to Shoppe.*

***

"Now, will the spirit understand time travel?" Axel asked Dracanna.

She stifled a yawn. She was getting tired of all the questions that the shamans were throwing at her. She wanted to get done with them, receive her permit and materials from Genghis, get her order for the table placed and get back to the shop. *The sooner I get myself and my crew off this desert planet, the better.*

"As I have said, the right spirit will possess the ability to *learn* how to travel through time. The odds are it won't know how the minute you bond it with the ship. There are tales of particularly good spirits that were able to take a ship into the time stream from the moment that they melded, but those are very rare, and I have never heard of a human spirit doing it."

"What kind of spirit will do it?" Axel was beginning to get on her nerves.

"A spirit that has been exposed to time travel in its mortal body will normally understand the ins and outs of controlling a ship."

"So, if you were to die, then your spirit would be able to travel through time as soon as it bonded with a ship." The stout shaman's eyes narrowed at her.

"Look, if you're thinking about killing me and sticking my soul in a ship, let me first tell you that like other parts of me, that's already spoken for." She pointed a sharp-nailed finger at Axel. *He's really starting to dance on my buttons.* "Nothing on this woman is available for any use you may have planned for it. Second. A soul has to have transitioned from the mortal plane for at least one standard

135

year. That means you'd be waiting for a while to make use of me, even if I was up for grabs. And third, if anything happens to me, my ship has the power to obliterate this planet and leave all of you little dirt fuckers floating in dust particles that she could gather up and use as toppings on sprinkle cones."

Axel paled. "I'm just trying to get a good idea of who we should call back for our first calling. Perhaps the spirit of a scout ship pilot would be better than a jockey."

The man was craftier than Dracanna gave him credit for. But then, he was apparently Genghis's chief shaman. That had to account for something in the way of intelligence. *You don't get so far up in the Mongol ranks just on cunning alone.* A scout ship pilot would be a perfect candidate, and would get the Mongolians off and flying faster than a land-based spirit would.

"How close are the controls of your new ships to your scout ships?" she asked. "If they are too different, there may be a bit of a learning curve. Going with someone who has no experience with space travel might be better, that way they wouldn't have anything to unlearn."

"I know a spirit of a scout ship pilot," No-Skins replied. None of the other shamans had offered their names to Dracanna, and she hadn't cared enough to ask. They were mostly quiet anyway. "A cousin of mine died while exploring a world on the rim a couple of years ago. We should be able to call him back to inhabit a ship."

"The rim is a very long way away," Dracanna started to object.

"Enough!" Axel shouted. "You have been seeking to delay us in acquiring your magic." He pulled a knife from his sash and stalked forward. "No more excuses. We will call the pilot into the first ship. You will show us the rituals

136

needed to complete the bonding process, and we will do it now!"

Dracanna glared as the stout man advanced toward her. "Well, if you want to take the extra time to call a spirit from light years away, fine. It won't be on my hands if this process takes longer than the Kahn thinks it should." She reached into her clutch and pulled out a pen and a piece of paper. She made a quick list of the things that she was going to need, then handed the paper to Axel.

"It's the middle of the night. I hope you guys have all this on hand, otherwise there'll be guards waking up the good citizens of Genghis looking for some of the more exotic things."

Axel snatched the list and read down it. He turned and thrust the list at one of the other skin-clad men. "Find these items. Quickly!"

Dracanna reclined against her pillows. *That should slow them down a bit.* She just hoped she could find other ways to foul the process. She didn't want to be the person responsible for unleashing Genghis Kahn on all of time and space. It was an effort not to think about her missing crew. After losing Rice Pilaf, she didn't want to lose Bea Man and Cat Astophe too. The cowboy she could explain away if the need came, but the others were known as her employees. She liked Dallas and wanted to be able to go back there soon.

***

"Are you sure about this?" Travis asked. "We don't know how Dracanna will act when we walk into the shop with a bunch of Grays in tow."

"Do you know anywhere else on this planet where we can get what we need to pull this off?" Conrad asked.

"Nope," Sassy answered for the cowboy. "I'd say

Dracanna's dressing room is the best place to go. I can even access the freezer."

"Good, then let's go." He turned toward the large crowd of Sasquatches and Insectoids that crowded behind the Grays. "We'll be back as quickly as we can. We should be able to launch the attack at dawn."

Travis slipped his large rough hand into Conrad's. "You know you really get me going when you go all Army-drill-sergeant on these guys."

"I was in the Air Force," Conrad replied as Sassy walked up to the doorway and made a couple of funny lines in chalk on the doorframe. The huge Bigfoot then tapped several times on the frame where he'd made the marks. The whole doorway shimmered, Sassy walked up to it and vanished.

"Might as well go, how much stranger can it be?" Conrad said, pulling Travis with him through the doorway, and out the freezer door of Scary Queen. The store was empty, other than Sassy walking toward the main door.

The cowbell clanked and the floor squeaked. A happy sensation washed over Conrad. Why he was happy to be back in the shop was beyond him, but somehow, it felt like he'd come home.

"I wonder where Dracanna and Bea are." Travis said as they walked far enough from the freezer to give the Grays room to clear the door.

"Dracanna, Bea, Scoop? Anyone here?" Conrad called.

"They're not here." Sassy came back from the door. "The door's locked too. Do you think you can do what we need, or are we going to have to wait for them to get back?"

"I can handle some of it, but all of this is new to me," Conrad replied. If there was no one there, it threw a kink

138

into his plan, or at least a delay. *Can I make things look as good as the experts could?* "Let's see what we can do." He looked over his shoulder, and the last of the thirty Gray ground troops cleared the freezer. With a sigh, he walked toward the back room, assuming they would follow.

As they entered the backroom he called for Scoop, again there was no answer. In his short time with the shop, the haunted implement had always been around. *It's possible that Dracanna took him along with her, or have Genghis Kahn and his men turned on her and captured them?* Travis's hand in his provided Conrad more comfort than he would have thought possible. At least he had someone from his own world with him as he led the aliens through the vastness of the small shop.

When he opened the door to the dressing room, several of the Grays stopped and stared. Thorial Five urged them forward. "We have all heard the rumors of the wonders of Darkholmian technologies. Don't let it worry you. The monsters of the dark lands will not descend to eat you."

"What is he talking about?" Travis whispered.

"A bit complicated to explain right now," Sassy said with a chuckle. "Catch me later about it."

On the far side of the dressing room, a door stood open to a lit corridor that Conrad didn't remember seeing before. He started toward it, when Bea's large red-headed figure charged out.

"Oh Gods, Conrad!" She swept him up in a huge bear hug, crushing him to her large fake bosom. "Shoppe has been so worried that she couldn't find you or Travis. Now Dracanna's missing too. But you two are back." She glanced over his shoulder at the line of Grays behind him. Her voice deepened "And you brought company."

"It's complicated," Conrad said, smoothing his blouse

and skirt back into place. "But with you here, we can get it all worked out."

"All what worked out?" Bea asked with an arched eyebrow. Her voice was slowly returning to normal.

"We're going to remake all these Grays into Mongolian women."

Bea stared at him for a minute. "I admit that the women on this planet aren't very pretty but you're asking for a miracle here. I love a challenge. However, I think I can do it. It's amazing what I can do with a bit of Avon, a touch of Maybelline, some Eva Gabor wigs and Lee Press-on nails."

***

"And you have the vessel prepared for the spirit?" Dracanna asked as she and the shamans waited for the one to return with the items necessary for them to call the spirit.

"You need not worry yourself about the ship," Axel said. "It's ready."

"Ah, the ship may be, but what about a vessel to hold the spirit once we call it?" Her dark eyebrows rose, and she tried to contain her humor at his misunderstanding.

Axel frowned. "I presumed that the ship itself was enough to contain the spirit."

"Would you want your crew treading all through the body of the spirit? If you try that, then it will soon come to begrudge the physicals that inhabit its body." Dracanna shook her head. "That never ends well. I presumed you were competent enough to have a spirit jar prepared. It needs to be something that fits into the central control panel."

"I told you there were things we didn't know about this," No-Skins said sharply. "Now we have to go and redesign the control panel to accommodate a spirit jar."

"No!" Axel spun on the lesser shaman. "We do not

have to redesign anything. We do not have time for that! The Kahn is ready for the next phase of his empire. We must not fail him in this." He glared at Dracanna. "You will prepare a spirit jar that will fit into the control panel as it is."

"But I'll need access to the special clay that Genghis has declared a controlled substance. To build a proper spirit jar, it takes proper clay. Do any of you happen to have some of the clay available?" *If this works, I'll acquire the clay, get it to the table maker and be able to delay giving them the knowledge they so desperately want. If I play my cards right, I might even be able to get The Scary Queen off planet before all hell breaks loose.*

The lead shaman sighed. "This had better not be a trick. What will it take to get the jar made?"

"Do any of you have a mystic kiln? We'll have to make sure that the clay is properly fired, or the spirit will be able to escape. You wouldn't want that now, would you?"

"There is only one mystic kiln in Genghis. How long will it take to complete the jar?"

Dracanna shrugged. "Hard to say, it depends on how busy the merchant with the kiln is." She didn't bother saying that she already knew he was backed up. Of course, an order from the Kahn himself would take precedence over ones ahead of it. *Can I get the table top into the same firing as the spirit jar?* Luckily the mystic clay dried faster than normal clay. "If there is only one kiln here right now, I believe I know the merchant running it. I'll be happy to take the clay to him."

"I can accompany you to the vendor," Axel snarled. "Send a guard to rouse the merchant." He instructed one of the other shamans while he rose from the cushions. "We'll go retrieve the clay that we need."

"Maybe after we get the ball rolling on this, I can stop

by my shop? There are some items that I need for my own personal comfort." Dracanna smiled, as her plan came together. *Now if everything at the Scary Queen was as I left it.*

6
Freedom Fried Ice

"See if you can find me something that looks more like native dresses than what we have on the racks," Bea instructed Conrad.

"But where else would we have anything?" he asked. For the past hour, Bea had been ordering him around while she set about applying various make ups and wigs to the Grays.

Bea sighed. "Go check with Scoop and see if he knows of anywhere Dracanna might have stashed a dozen Mongolian women's outfits."

"Where's Scoop?" Conrad had been wondering where the implement was, but they'd been so busy trying to turn the Grays into a bunch of human women that he'd forgotten to ask.

"Oh, he should be on the bridge of the Darkholmian ship."

"And where is that?"

"Through the open door there." She paused in her application of eyebrows and pointed the eyebrow pencil toward the doorway she'd walked through an hour ago. "Go down the hallway. You can't miss it."

"I can go," Travis piped up from the pile of wig boxes he was digging through.

"Nope, you know where you are in that mess," Bea objected. "We need four more dark brunette or black wigs for our friends here."

Travis' big shoulders slumped as he opened the next box.

"Be back as soon as I can." Conrad headed for the hallway.

The inside of the Darkholmian ship was eerie. Soft lights illuminated the gloom, but only enough so he could find his way down the desolate hallway without banging into the walls. A few closed doors lined the space every now and then, but he ignored them. There was a brighter glow ahead of him. He focused on that. *I hope I'm not just heading to the light at the end of the tunnel.*

Lights of various colors, but mostly reds and oranges, illuminated the room he entered. A series of control panels, that looked more like what he thought a spaceship's panels should look like, were spread out before him. In the center, a chair sat, waiting for an occupant.

"Scoop, you in here?" he called out. His voice echoed in the Spartan confines of the room.

"Over here, Conrad," the implement's voice came from the chair. As he moved the couple of steps toward it, Conrad wondered how the thing managed to make a directional sound when it had no mouth, but figured he'd wait until a better time to ask the silly question.

"Hey Scoop, Bea sent me to see if you happen to know if we have any Mongolian women's clothes stashed anywhere. We need enough to cover up a dozen Grays."

"So that's why Shoppe said you had returned with a

bunch of Grays in tow. You're disguising them to sneak into Genghis's stronghold. I presume they want to rescue Gyre."

He looked down into the chair at where Scoop leaned against the arm, metal touching metal. "That's right."

"It's about time someone did something for that poor creature."

"So, do you know if Dracanna has any clothing available?"

"Not Mongolian. It's not her style. But I bet I can help out a bit. This ship has a duplicator system. It's fairly simple, can't handle complex non-mundane things, but it should do clothes just fine. Like so much of things in here, it's been disabled, but I think I can get it going again. The thing is, we'll need raw materials to put in to get things out."

"Raw materials?" Conrad went to lean against the nearest control panel facing the chair.

"Wait, don't lean there!" Scoop shouted. "I just got that panel working from the chair."

Conrad straightened. "Sorry."

"I caught you in time, so there's no problem. Now, we can use anything we have since the duplicator system works on taking one thing and turning it into something else. Sort of like a 3D printer, but more complex. We'll have to use your skirt and blouse as a master. You can adjust the color and texture a bit, but the cut will be identical, the system isn't very creative. Like I said, nothing very complex about it."

"What kinds of things can we use?" Conrad wasn't sure he just wanted to go through either ship grabbing things, he had no idea if they were useful or not, to be raw materials for the duplicator. "Hey how about the tables that got busted in the tumble through space?"

"Those would work wonderfully, and anything else

that got broken can go in too," Scoop replied. "The duplicator is two doors down on the right. It's an odd looking contraption, but I'll go ahead and get the power on in that room and get it booted up for you."

"Good, I'll go get Travis and have him and Sassy help me drag stuff in there." He started out the door. "Do you think I could duplicate me some better clothes? This skirt is so not me."

Scoop laughed. "If you can find anything suitable." Then the implement fell silent for a moment. "Shoppe again has a reading on Dracanna. She has come out of Genghis' compound. If we're lucky, things are looking up a bit."

***

The ceramic merchant stared over the counter at Dracanna and Axel with bleary unfocused eyes. The guard that had woken the poor man up for their visit stood at the door, his arms folded over his broad chest.

"For the Kahn, of course everything will be set aside." The man's voice shook slightly. Dracanna couldn't tell if it were from lack of sleep or fear of Axel and Genghis. "But it will be six hours before the kiln can be opened, otherwise the magic will have to be reset, and that will take most of the day."

Axel slammed his fist down on the counter, causing the man to jump. "And how long will the firing take once the items are in the kiln?"

"The jar will be more delicate than the tables, of course. But they'll all be fired together. They'll be ready when the store opens day after tomorrow."

"That'll be fine," Dracanna replied, putting a restraining black nailed hand on Axel's shoulder. "It'll give us time to be well rested before using the jar."

"Make sure there are no mistakes in your work," Axel

growled at the merchant. He then turned on his heels and stomped out of the building.

"Thanks," Dracanna said with a smile before she followed the shaman.

"The Kahn will not be pleased with this development." Axel stormed off down the deserted dusty lane between the mix of adobe buildings and closed yurts.

"It's a delay that cannot be helped." Dracanna said, her long stride allowing her to easily keep pace with the man.

The shaman stopped and rounded on her. "Are you sure you didn't plan this?"

Dracanna rolled her eyes and resisted the urge to punch the little man. *Like any of the problems they were encountering could possibly be my fault.* Sure, she was used to puppeting royal courts to do her bidding, but she hadn't planned on coming to Mongoleon, let alone getting caught up in Genghis's bid to expand his already vast empire. With her crew still missing, she really wanted to take her frustration out on somebody. Axel was a good target, but it would make him difficult to work with in the future.

"Oh go throw some bones or something and divine that I had nothing to do with any of this." She sighed. "Is it my fault that you and your people knew so little about what you were doing with the spirit summoning that you didn't know you needed a magically constructed spirit jar to hold the spirit that would be piloting the ship? So you really think I would do something so foolish as to have my own people kidnapped while at Genghis' dinner party? I understand you people have a good reason to be paranoid about everything, but come on; you're looking at the wrong woman to find behind your conspiracy theories. Now, why don't you run along and explain to Genghis that it'll be tomorrow before we can make any more advance on his little time invasion, and I'll return to my shop and freshen up a bit. A girl needs her beauty rest, and you can't expect me to cast the complex spells we need if I don't get my sleep." She didn't bother explaining that as a Darkholmian, she didn't need sleep the same way humans did. It was a little more information than she wanted to reveal. What she really wanted to do was get back to the shop and figure a way out, before she had to show the shamans the spell.

"Fine, go!" he snapped. "We know where the Scary Queen is currently parked. Do not try to leave the planet. Genghis has ordered his space ships to fire on you should you attempt to depart without his permission." Axel resumed his stomp down the lane, toward the heart of Genghis.

Dracanna spun on her heels and headed toward the Scary Queen, hoping Scoop or Bea would have some good news about finding Cat and Travis. *Somehow, things have got to improve, but at least I have a day and a half before I have to put the next fly in their facial cream. Now, I just have to find the right fly and the right cream.*

***

"Are you sure we have time for this?" Travis asked Conrad, a strange, almost sexy look on his rugged face.

"Sure," Conrad replied. "We have to use the machine to churn out clothes for the Grays, and Scoop didn't say I couldn't make a few for myself while I was at it. We might make some for you too. I really want to ditch the skirts for a while." He didn't bother adding forever.

Travis laughed, and his face relaxed. "You sure this isn't just an attempt to see my body?"

Blood rushed to Conrad's face. Thankfully, no one but Travis was currently in the duplicator room with him.

"I take that as a yes," Travis said. He caught Conrad

148

up in his arms and kissed him. The kiss was deeper and warmer than the one they'd shared in the Gray compound earlier. "If things weren't so crazy right now, all you'd have to do was ask the right way. That is, as long as I get to see a bit more of your skin too."

"I guess since we're going to use the stuff I'm wearing now as a template for the Grays, you'll get that chance," Conrad replied. They'd already hauled in several shattered tables and a few other things that had obviously been broken by their roller coaster ride through spacetime. Just to be on the safe side, they'd checked with Bea to make sure they weren't mistaking perfectly good, but odd items for damaged stuff.

Conrad pulled the Mongolian blouse over his head and placed it in the original item tube on the machine's right side.

"Not bad," Travis said, resting a large hand on Conrad's now bare shoulder.

"Since I left the Air Force, I still try to work out from time to time," he replied. "Now Scoop said this thing basically works like a copy machine, put an original item in the one side, hit a button, and get a duplicate out the other side. He said something about being able to adjust color if I wanted to but all this stuff looks alike anyway, so why bother?" He hit the biggest button, it had DUP in big bold letters. But the letters changed before his eyes, as if his brain was somehow allowing him to read the alien text that kept popping up. *This has to be another part of that translator stuff Dracanna made us eat. I can read alien as well as speak and understand it. If it wasn't so cool, it would be freaky.*

The machine buzzed and a noxious stink seeped out of the left-hand tube. Conrad backed up and bumped into

Travis. The cowboy wrapped his arms around Conrad and pulled him close. For the first time in almost two days, Conrad felt safe. With that safety, came exhaustion. They'd been on the go for nearly forty eight hours without sleep, other than their time in the cocoons. While the duplicator replicated his blouse, he leaned back against Travis, enjoying the feel of the man's strong body against his naked back. Neither said a word while the rancid yellow goo solidified into a perfect copy of the blouse.

Not wanting to leave the comfort of Travis' arms, Conrad forced himself to step up to the tube and extract the new garment. It looked and felt exactly like the original. He set the machine to make eleven more blouses, then eased back into Travis's embrace to watch the gelatinous spectacle unfold.

Travis kissed the back of Conrad's neck. He wished they had more time; he would've enjoyed exploring the man, even on this strange new world. Shoving the heavy Mongolian skirt to the floor, he gave a sigh to be free of the women's clothing, if just for a little while. Seconds later, Travis's big hands cupped his butt through his boxer briefs.

Conrad chuckled and leaned heavier against Travis as the third blouse dropped from the tube onto the metal floor near the skirt. "We really don't have time to get anything started right now."

Travis chuckled back. "I know, and I really don't want Thorial Five coming in to observe our mating habits."

"I don't know; we might be able to show him how anal probing is supposed to be done. His future subjects might appreciate that. They say you can't be a good top without first being a good bottom." Conrad turned in Travis's embrace so he could kiss the man, which didn't help the growing urgency that was already straining his briefs.

The duplicator beeped.

"Hey you two," Bea's voice came from the doorway. "Ah…I think I'll give you a couple of minutes."

Inwardly, Conrad groaned as their lips separated. "We don't have a couple of minutes Bea. What's up?" He carefully kept his body pressed against Travis to hide his arousal, but turned his head toward her.

"Just checking to see how you guys are progressing on getting those outfits together."

"I think the blouses are done," he replied. "Just need to get the skirt into the machine."

"Well, that explains your showing off that hot bod to the cowboy," Bea said with a chuckle. "Well, just bring everything in as soon as you can. Thorial is getting antsy to get going, and I don't want him scratching at the makeup and ruining my hard work. Do you have any idea how difficult it is to make those Grays look remotely human? There is only so much that I can do with the limited amount of foundation we have on hand."

"Be there as soon as we can," he replied.

"Good, and don't get any stains that show up under black light on the new clothes." Then Bea disappeared down the hallway.

Conrad reluctantly pulled out of Travis' embrace and stepped over to the machine. He took out the blouse and put in the skirt to start the process again. Not ready to cover himself from Travis' gaze, he laid the blouse over the control panel.

"So do you think I have a hot bod too?" he asked as he walked back toward the cowboy.

Travis smiled. "Yeah, I do." He pulled his Mongolian tunic over his head, revealing his massive chest with a

151

dusting of blond hair. His blue eyes sparkled. "So what do you think of mine?"

"Oh, definitely hot," Conrad said with a smile as his fingers caressed Travis. Then he pulled back. "Man we can't keep this up. We've got to get these clothes duplicated and get this game on the road. But I promise you, when this whole thing is over, when we've defeated Genghis Kahn, freed the captive Gray and the universe, I am so jumping your hot bod."

"I'll hold you to that." Travis said, capturing his hand before he could move too far away. He brought it up to his lips and kissed Conrad's long fingers. "Maybe we can see who jumps whom the fastest when this is over."

A wide, shit-eating grin split Conrad's face. "Deal!"

***

Something felt different as Dracanna unlocked the Scary Queen's door. Someone had been in her store. A wave of happiness from Shoppe told her she'd been missed. It was one of the positive things about having a spirit controlling the ship as opposed to an AI. An AI couldn't miss you. It could acknowledge your absence or presence, but it didn't actually miss you the way a person or a spirit could. In some ways, coming home to Shoppe was a lot like coming home to a dog that was happy to see you.

"Something's going on isn't it, girl?" she asked. "Scoop! I'm back!" she called out.

There was no reply. The row of incandescent lights flickered in a line toward the back room.

"Thanks, Shoppe," Dracanna said and followed the lights. As she passed the standing merchandise freezers, she noticed that one of the doors was ajar—the door to the portal freezer. *Great, now what has come through?*

Lights glowed in the back room, but there was no one

there. The door to the storeroom was open, as was the dressing room door. Sounds of conversation came from the latter. Bea was talking to someone; it sounded like she was doing their hair, while subtle undertones rang out from several more subdued discussions.

Dracanna stopped in the doorway and stared into the dressing room. Standing around, were what appeared to be eleven really skinny women in Mongolian dress. Their hair wasn't right; then she realized they were all wearing wigs, most of them wigs that Rice Pilaf had used, straight dark coifs of various lengths. Then one of them lifted a long delicate hand. *Grays!*

"What in all the Hells is going on in here?" she asked at the top of her voice. The diminutive aliens spun to look her, their large eyes glowing in concern.

Bea looked over her broad shoulder toward the door. "About time you got back. We've got to get busy if we're going to get done before dawn. Now get over here and lend me a hand. Neither Cat nor Travis is any help whatsoever with makeup, and these…folks need a lot of makeup."

"I repeat, what is going on here?" Dracanna stomped past the staring Grays toward her red-haired employee.

"Maybe I can shed some light on the situation," Sassy stepped out of the shadows.

"You know I never did buy your silent act." Dracanna glared at the Sasquatch. "I've known others of your kind that had no problem at all talking. You're actually all rather easy to understand, particularly within the translation spells I put in my special confections."

A row of white teeth shown from the shaggy face. "Like I told Conrad, it made Bea flirt with me more."

"So, I take it you're not here for flirting?" Dracanna put a hand on her hip and stared up at the big biped.

"Nope, we're here for war." Sassy sounded rather calm, considering what he had just said. "Conrad and Travis agreed to help us overthrow Genghis, and Bea's lending a hand too."

"They what!?!" Dracanna roared.

"Whoa now." Bea stopped teasing a wig that sat awkwardly on a gray head. "You know we're doing the right thing. These people have been oppressed by him for way too long. It's about time someone did something to stop him."

Dracanna paused and took a deep breath, before she continued. *Wasn't I thinking that same thing as I dealt with the shamans? But I want to be off world,* now. *I don't want to get caught up in a very dangerous situation.* "Yes, but we've got places to be," she objected weakly.

"Oh please, Bitch," Bea said. "We have a time machine at our disposal. We got nowhere to be fast. Besides, we have to help Thorial Five rescue Meridia Twelve from Genghis' cage."

Dracanna shook her head. "What are you going on about? Genghis only has one Gray and that's Gyre."

"Yeah," Bea said with a nod, "her real name is Meridia Twelve. She was Thorial's mate. We'll be helping reunite lovers who've been apart for over two thousand years." She paused and placed a hand dramatically on her chest. "I know their tale touched my heart."

"Every lost love story touches your dried up heart. Aren't you the one that went on about that story about the silly teen girl who killed herself because her boyfriend left her?"

"Yeah, but she came back as a vampire, and they lived happily ever after with their little vampire babies. This will be a lot better ending." She started teasing the wig again.

"Dracanna, dark lady," one of the Grays approached her. It was taller and broader than the other ones. The wig on its head actually sat in a normal position and the brown blouse it wore didn't sag on its shoulders very badly. "I am Thorial Five. I humbly beseech you to aid me in the quest to get Meridia Twelve back. It has been too long that the tyrant has held her captive. You would be doing myself and the entire universe a great favor. The Grays would be forever in your debt."

Dracanna frowned. "I need to discuss it with my crew. Bea, where are Cat Astrophe and that cowboy?"

"Still on the ship, they are supposed to be using the duplicator to make clothes."

"Wait, how did they get access to the ship?" Her heart stopped for a moment. *What if they'd run afoul of the AI controlling the Darkholmian ship?* Then she realized who was still missing from her crew. "And where's Scoop?"

***

Conrad pulled the Mongolian tunic over his head. Being copied from Travis', it hung a bit large on him, but the rougher cloth felt welcome against his skin after the flimsy silk that the blouse had been. He grabbed a belt and wrapped it around his waist.

"Looks better on you than the blouse did," Travis said, after pulling his own tunic back on.

Conrad felt sorry to see the man's magnificent body disappear, but hoped he'd get time to explore it more after they were off planet. "Thanks, now let's go check in with Scoop and see if there's anything he needs."

"You know it's odd thinking of an ice-cream scoop as he, or even living, for that point." Travis pulled his boots on before they headed out the door.

"I know. This whole thing is a lot more than I

155

bargained for. All I wanted was a job, not an adventure."

Travis laughed. "What was that old slogan for the military, it's not a job, it's an adventure."

Conrad frowned as they stepped out into the hallway. "That was Army. In the Air Force, we flew higher."

"I'm just a little ole Texas farm boy," Travis said with a sexy grin. "Never could keep it straight which was which."

The door to the command room still stood open, and the soft lights continued to illuminate the command chair.

"Hey, Scoop, how you doing in here?" Conrad asked as they walked up behind the chair.

"Almost got through to the AI," Scoop replied. "Just need a little more push." The soft light of the room blazed chasing all the shadows from the room.

"There are intruders on board," a mechanical voice announced at a loud volume.

"We reactivated you!" Scoop shouted.

The door slammed shut. "Two humans, and one animate. Remove all the humans and the animate is not an issue."

"Shoppe, we need a hand here!" Scoop screamed.

Conrad and Travis turned and looked for a way to reopen the door.

"There has to be a knob, switch or something here," Travis said, his big hands sliding along the left side of the door.

"Nothing here," Conrad mirrored the cowboy's actions on the right side. "Scoop, open the door!"

"Trying, the AI is fighting me for control," he replied. "Shoppe is trying to override it."

"Beginning removal of the human infestation of the ship."

"We are not an infestation!" Conrad shouted,

pounding his fist into the metal wall. A loud clang filled the small command room.

The lights in the room dimmed for a moment, then brightened back up. "Darkholmian override accepted. Counter measures cancelled. System returning to normal."

"What in the hell?" Conrad asked as he rubbed his sore knuckles. A loud click came from the door, and it slid open. Dracanna and Bea stood there staring at them.

***

Dracanna drew a steadying breath as the door opened. She hoped she was in time to save Cat and Travis. Luckily, the newer AIs still accepted her as part of the Darkholmian royal family and all defaulted to her voice commands. She'd have to ask her father, or whoever she found to talk to when she got there, how they had her new voice print. Like most transsexuals, her voice was different than it had been as a man. It hadn't gotten higher, just rougher. *Did I just admit that I'm heading to Darkholme once we're done here?*

"Scoop, are you in there?" she asked as she cleared the threshold.

"Are we glad to see you," Cat said. The big cowboy stood just off to his side with a look of relief plastered on his face. Cat was now in male Mongolian garb.

Dracanna sighed. She wondered if this was part of the plan. "What are you three up to?"

"We were just getting the AI turned back on," Scoop replied. "For some reason Wren had disabled it."

"There might have been a good reason for him to do that," Dracanna said, stepping alongside the chair. "Some of these new AIs are buggier than windows ME was. Did you think of that?"

"No." Scoop sounded like if he'd had a head, it would've been bowed.

"I take it Shoppe had to interface with it to get it going again?"

"That's right."

The mistress of the Scary Queen picked up Scoop and sat down in the command chair.

"Don't do that!" Bea shouted. "It will constrict around you."

Again Dracanna sighed. "Bea, you of all people should know not to take alien tech for granted. This chair, like most Darkholmian command chairs, is programmed to react whenever someone who is not a vampire sits down in it, or someone it has not been programmed to accept. It didn't have your bio print on file, so it reacted. How did you get free?"

"Scoop and Shoppe managed to override it," Bea replied.

"I'm impressed, Scoop," Dracanna said. "I wasn't sure you still have enough Darkholmian in you to pull off accessing one of these newer ships."

"Shoppe helped."

"I'm sure she did." Dracanna's black nails tapped on Scoop's bowl. "Now that it's all handled, I want to know what in the many Hells you people are planning to do with all the Grays that are in the dressing room, and how does that work into overthrowing Genghis."

"We actually haven't figured out how to overthrow Genghis," Cat spoke up. "Our plan right now is to get into the citadel, release Meridia Twelve, get out and then have the Sasquatches get all the Grays off planet as quickly as possible."

"As quickly as possible," she mimed. "Yeah, that was my plan too. I wanted all of us off this misbegotten dust bowl as quickly as possible. We're waiting for a table to get made, then hopefully, if Genghis doesn't pull something, we can get out of here."

"But what about Meridia Twelve?" Cat asked.

Bea walked around to the front of the chair and glared down at her employer. "Look, your Bitchiness, you said a little while ago we could help out with this. What's with the change of plan now?"

Dracanna continued drumming on Scoop. "I didn't say anything about changing plans. We need to figure out how we're going to overthrow a tyrant that rules a quarter of the known galaxy and get out of it with our skins intact. I've had about enough of Genghis and his plans for conquest."

"Okay, so what did he do this time?" Bea asked, still staring down her broad nose. "You've gotten mad at him before, but always just left and not worried about him. Now?"

"Now, he's trying to get Darkholmian tech out of me." She stopped drumming. "I *will not be* the person responsible for unleashing that tyrant on the whole of spacetime. So, I guess that means we have to find a way to stop him. I've delayed his shamans the best I can. If we can do something between now and tomorrow morning, that would be preferable."

"We're going into his citadel this morning for Meridia Twelve," Conrad said, stepping around to the right hand side of the chair. "If you can come up with something before we go, then let's get two jobs done in one raid."

"What are our assets?" Dracanna never liked to make plans without knowing what she had going for her. The harder the situation, the more assets she wanted.

"We have over a hundred Insectoids ready to cause as much of a disturbance as we need," explained Cat. "There may be more coming from other hives, we're not sure yet on the total numbers. They'll be here about daybreak. We've got the strike force of twelve Grays that we're getting prepared, and another fifty ready to go from the outside. Sassy managed to round up seventy-eight of his people, also raring to go. They'll also provide getaway if things get out of hand."

Dracanna nodded. "I'm impressed, Conrad." She stopped, realizing it was the first time she'd used his masculine name since they'd given him a drag name. "You have a good head on your shoulders. You've been thrown into a situation, the likes of which most humans have never dreamed of outside of cheap Science Fiction movies. In working with the Grays, Insectoids, and Sasquatches, you're dealing with creatures that don't even appear human. And through this, you're holding up just fine. I can see why Shoppe likes you. You have a lot of potential. Now, if we can just get you to keep your dress on, everything will be great."

"Thanks…I think," Conrad replied.

"Take the compliment," Travis whispered into the man's ear, but Dracanna still managed to hear it.

"You're coping pretty well with this yourself, cowboy," she continued. "So what do you plan to be doing while Conrad and his troops of aliens and monsters are off rescuing the fair Gray damsel?"

"I'm going with him," Travis said, puffing out his chest. "He might need me."

The realization hit her and Dracanna smiled. "You're in love with him aren't you?"

"We just met two nights ago," Conrad objected.

Dracanna held up her hand and turned to look at Travis in the face, her eyes bore into his, the blackness of them sucking deep into his blue depts. "That's why you're doing this, isn't it? There is something about our Conrad here that you've fallen in love with." Part of Travis' soul recoiled at her touch, but she pulled him toward her, yanking at him in a way she hadn't yanked on anyone in a long time. He physically bent toward the chair. It had been centuries since she'd even accidentally used her formidable mental powers on a human mind. The sensation strengthened her for the coming battle.

"I think so," he whispered. Dracanna felt the fear in him at letting this bit of information out. She marveled that humans, who were so open with their ignorance, were so closed with their emotions.

"Dracanna, leave him alone!" Bea touched her arm, breaking her contact with the man. "Travis is a nice young man. He doesn't deserve this from you."

Scoop chilled in her grasp. "Be nice, Dracanna."

She ran a hand through her long black hair. "I'm just making sure we understand his motives. Conrad might need protecting on this. Travis is perfect for that. Can you shoot, cowboy?"

Travis blinked and looked unsure about answering. "Yeah, of course I can shoot."

"Pistol, rifle, shotgun?"

He straightened his broad shoulders. "Yeah, all of them."

"Good, we'll find the weapons locker on this ship and get you armed for Mongolian bear."

"You know, I saw one of those riding bears at the market this afternoon."

Conrad laid a hand on Travis's arm. "Look, we get through this, and we'll see about finding you a bear to ride."

Dracanna put both hands on the arms of the command chair. "AI, I am Dracanna of the royal house of Dragon's, rulers of Darkholme, to whom am I speaking?"

"Voice print accepted," the mechanical voice replied. "This is Pal, I am a seventh generation AI from the Darkholme forges."

"Pal, do you know why Wren turned you off?"

Bea waved a hand as the computer answered.

"I disagreed with his plans for our mission. He disabled me before we could contact you."

"Hey boss, if we're done with most of the immediate stuff here, I got some Grays to finish transforming." Bea said before she walked out.

"We should go too." Conrad grabbed Travis arm with a look of relief as he moved to follow.

"I'll be out shortly," Dracanna replied without looking up from where her eyes were now fixed on a red blinking light dominating the center of the control panel to her right.

"What was your disagreement about?" she asked. The red light blinked faster as the AI responded.

"He did not wish to honor the orders we were given."

"Which were?"

The red light paused for a moment, then blinked again. "To return you and any of your companions to Darkholme. No one was to be harmed."

Dracanna nodded. "And he was prepared to harm us?" That was obvious given what he'd done to Rice, but she wanted to see what the AI had to say for itself.

"Yes."

"Why did you not follow the orders of the commander of the vessel?"

"My service is first and foremost to the royal house of Darkholme." The light blinked wildly. "You outrank him. My service is to you."

Dracanna couldn't tell how, but she knew the AI had

just lied.

**

Conrad relaxed as they walked down the hall, but he didn't let go of Travis' arm. "Damn, she can be scary."

"Why do you think we call her the Scary Queen?" Bea replied.

"I thought that was the name of the shop," Travis said, patting Conrad's hand.

The contact felt good. Conrad wondered for a moment if Dracanna had really just forced a confession of love out of Travis, or had he just answered to get her to leave him alone.

Bea chuckled. "Oh honey, the shop has been called many things across many different worlds. I can't even remember what it was called when I joined the crew, but I quickly figured out that Dracanna can be a very scary queen when she wants to be, and that seemed like a perfect name when Shoppe changed into its current incarnation and needed a new name. Yeah, her Bitchiness objected, but Scoop and I, along with the other crew at the time, overruled her. I think Shoppe likes it too."

That gave Conrad the opening to ask a question that had been eating at him since they found Rice dead. "Bea, what happened to all the other employees?"

"Well, most of them went on with their lives over time. They found reasons to leave. Some of them fell in love and settled down. Some of them just got tired of never knowing where we were going to get dragged off to next, and some…like poor Rice, died. But she was the first one to die on the job."

They walked the rest of the way to the dressing room in silence. Conrad wasn't sure if the revelation made him feel better or worse. For a moment, it cast a dark pall over him as they prepared to save poor Gyre.

7
Baked Mongolian

Dracanna pushed a long lock of black hair out of her face. She didn't like the ideas Conrad and the aliens had come up with, but couldn't think of anything better. Overthrowing an existing regime was always a tricky proposition, and it went against her need to stay neutral in the universe she traversed. If her table was going to be finished soon enough, she would've just thrown the aliens out of the shop, locked her employees up and waited a few hours for it all to blow up or blow over, but she couldn't leave the planet in time. Conrad had given his word to help the Grays and since she still hadn't figured out what it was about the man that Shoppe liked so much, she couldn't figure out how to avoid the situation without upsetting her sentient spaceship. So, she was stuck playing out her role in their overthrow of the largest empire the galaxy had ever known. At least she had to agree the tyrant had outlived his usefulness. Now, hopefully, she'd get everyone to be quiet about her involvement. *I don't want it getting out that I'm willing to help overthrow folks. It might be bad for business.*

The flap to Genghis's massive yurt opened as she

approached. The intergalactic despot stood there, waiting, as he did every morning for the rising sun. For over two thousand years, the man greeted the sun as it crested the horizon. A slight smile graced Dracanna's painted lips. *Little does he know that this is liable to be the last sun he welcomes.*

"Genghis," Dracanna stepped around the guards that watched them both with sharp eyes. "Looks like the start of a most auspicious day."

He shrugged. "Does it? My people tell me it will still be a couple of days before they can complete work on my own version of your marvelous Shoppe."

"Why don't you come walk with me?" She offered her arm to him. "We have time to move beyond the confines of town before the sun is completely up. How long has it been since you welcomed the day in without all the tents in the way? We can use the time to talk. I think you'll be interested in what I have to tell you."

He cocked his head slightly as he accepted her arm. "Have you decided it's time to divulge more of your secrets to me? I have heard some of the rumors of turmoil on Darkholme. You know, together we can take back your throne. Think of the force we could be." Two of the guards moved from the entrance of his yurt to follow as they strolled toward the edge of Genghis town.

Dracanna released a tightly controlled laugh. *Does he really think I'd be foolish enough to unleash him on even more of the universe than he currently controls?* "Yes, those rumors have reached me too, but trust me when I say, I still want nothing to do with my father or the mess he has created on Darkholme." *Even if that will be my next stop after leaving Mongoleon, unless I can find some way of killing Wren and destroying his ship. And unfortunately*

Darkholmian ships are nearly impossible to destroy.

"Then you won't mind if I set my sights there while it's in a state of disarray?" He sounded hopeful.

"As long as you leave me out of the conflict," she replied. "All I want to do now is get Shoppe running again and resume my rounds. There are a lot of people out in the galaxy waiting for the treats I bring them."

"If you aren't ready to divulge more of your secrets, why have you come this morning?" A note of suspicion entered his voice.

"I am still distressed by the loss of my crew," she lied. "It's been more than a day. I was hoping your people would've come up with something." The predawn light grew brighter. The sun would be peeking over the horizon any minute. She hoped to have him a little further from the yurt before that happened. Dracanna lengthened her stride, and he stepped up to match it.

"As you are well aware, my shamans have been otherwise occupied. The guards are working with what they can. Once my shamans have finished the job they and you are working on, they can turn their attention to finding your crew."

"But I thought maybe one of your orbiting ships might be able to scan for the insects. Surely your sensors can find them. Mine were damaged in the flight here."

"If I had any of my ships in orbit right now, it would be simple for them to find the rebel bugs, but I have dispatched all my ships toward Darkholme." A triumphant tone colored his voice. She'd known him long enough to know Genghis Kahn loved taking over new territory and subjecting the people there to his iron will.

There was something about the timing of it all. *Was this why the Grays and Inscetoids picked this time to try and*

*overthrow Genghis? Most of his ships are out of the sector.
If he's here, then who's leading the attack force?*

***

Sweat rolled down Conrad's back as they stood in the shadows a couple of yurts down from Genghis' central home. Hopefully his makeup would hold up to his nerves. His skirt was tighter than he remembered it being. He thought it was arrogant of the leader to have left the safety of his bunker already. With the attack only a day before, anyone in his right mind would've stayed in the fortified place until he was sure the danger had passed. But he'd returned to the ceremonial yurt that had been breached once already.

"There they go," Travis said. The cowboy had been watching for Dracanna and Genghis to leave the yurt. "They got two guards with them."

"Good," Bea said. "That's fewer we have to get past." She turned toward the Grays behind them. "You guys just stick to the plan. Let me do all the talking."

Thorial Five nodded. His straight, dark wig nearly slid off his head. For some reason, even an ample application of spirit gum wouldn't hold the wigs to the Grays' skin. They all had to move very carefully to keep the wigs on. Conrad had asked if they had any burkas on board, thinking that the heavy clothing worn by Muslim women might resolve the problem, but Dracanna had been fast to point out that Mongolians weren't Muslims and that burkas were *not* something any inhabitant of Mongoleon would wear. Unfortunately it was the wrong season for heavy hats, so the Grays were stuck with trying to keep their heads level to maintain their disguises as they walked.

With Bea in the lead, they headed out in a line while Conrad ever watchfully brought up the rear. Several of the

Grays carried large wicker baskets, a couple had brooms, and Conrad and Travis carried mops. Hopefully, the regular cleaning crew hadn't been in yet to remove the chaos of the party, and they could get past the guards with little or no trouble. With only four men in front of the yurt now, if there was a problem, they might be able to overpower them before they raised the alarm.

"The Khan requested clean up first thing this morning," Bea said, her voice shifting to have a somewhat native accent.

The guard barely looked up at them. "Go on in," he ordered.

Conrad breathed a little easier as they filed between the guards on either side of the yurt flap. It still amazed him that someone as powerful as Genghis Khan primarily lived in a tent and had very little security around him. But this was his new home planet and he kept everyone down with a tight fist.

The tent was still a complete disaster. The central table had been overturned. Where he'd been seated, a tunnel, just large enough for Travis' broad shoulders, ran down through torn rugs and soil. Several more tunnels opened into the room, presumably where the other guests that had been taken had sat. Most of the chairs and cushions were overturned, along with smaller tables. The remains of the feast they'd partaken of lay scattered about amidst shards of broken pottery and shattered glass.

I can't believe nobody thought to follow the tunnels down to find us, or maybe they did and things down there just got messy. "I'm glad we don't actually have to clean up this disaster area," Conrad said.

"Me too," Travis agreed. "But where's Meridia Twelve? The cage behind Genghis' chair is empty."

168

Conrad looked at the golden cage where last he'd seen the captive Gray. It was bare.

"I can sense her," Thorial Five said. "She is near."

***

"So Genghis, I thought you always lead the attacks personally." Dracanna said.

The intergalactic tyrant sighed. "I thought this would be a good opportunity for my youngest son to get his blade bloodied. His mother says I've been too controlling and need to let him try his own hand. I sent my best advisors along with him."

Dracanna nodded. *So that's where most of his cabinet are. I wondered about that at dinner.* "How many children do you have, Genghis? I've lost count over the years."

"Legitimate or total?" he asked with a chuckle. "You know I've bred enough bastards to populate a planet or four. If you just asked, I'd be happy to provide you with one of your own."

She didn't have to pretend to be mortified. "You know Darkholmians and humans can't reproduce." *Not that I could if I wanted to, by any method, natural or otherwise.*

He laughed loudly as they cleared the yurts on the edge of the capital. "And you know that I haven't been completely human in over two thousand years. Thanks to my dear Gray, Gyre, I think I could probably father children on any species I wanted. Some of the Gray gene-splicing techniques are extremely impressive."

"I know they are, but wasn't aware that you had used any of them on yourself, other than to make yourself ageless." The thought of Genghis gaining the genetic gifts of some of the other races terrified her. He was scary enough as a human, being more was horrific.

They paused as the sun crested the horizon. Genghis

stood there, silent, intent on the golden orb's arrival. Dracanna had never completely lost her fear of suns. On her own world, the blue sun would turn her to dust. Thankfully there weren't a lot of habitable worlds in the universe that had blue suns. Her kind were safe from other light, the ultraviolet rays weren't as strong and thus, not deadly to them. But the instinctive urge to be protected from sunlight had been bred into her species for millions of years and was hard to ignore. The term 'blue light special' always made her flinch.

"My dear Dracanna," he said finally, turning away from the sun and looking at her. His face was more at peace than she could remember seeing it in a long time. "There is so much more to life than immortality."

The sand under their feet exploded as a swarm of insectoid warriors surfaced in front of them. They were both knocked down.

***

"Where is she?" Conrad asked, looking around for any sign of the captive Gray.

"Near," Thorial replied. "It's almost like she's trying to hide herself from me. Like she's ashamed."

"How about through there?" Travis pointed to a curtain that cut off part of the yurt. "Maybe that's his private quarters or something."

Bea hurried ahead. "Good thinking, sweetie! I knew you were more than just a pretty face." She shoved the curtain aside.

The room was more spartan than the dining area. A single bed, just a cot really, rested against the far wall covered in an ornate blanket of blues and golds. A simple chair sat next to a massive wooden wardrobe. Across from it, a large golden cage held a small pale figure. Meridia

170

Twelve looked over her shoulder at them as they entered. Tears streamed from her huge eyes and poured off her narrow chin.

"No!" she wailed, her voice high and distraught.

***

Sand flew as the warriors erupted around them. As she picked herself up from the dirt, they reminded Dracanna of Hindu Gods with weapons in their many arms. Like an angry hive of army ants, they flowed over the dictator. She jumped away just in time to save herself from being taken down with him.

Genghis remained eerily silent, although his two guards screamed war cries as they dove for the attackers. Those cries were cut short as several Insectoids turned on them and hacked them down in bright sprays of blood. The sight reminded Dracanna that she hadn't fed on real blood in months.

The pile of Insectoids covering Genghis shook, then flew backwards. A wave of mental energy passed over Dracanna. It raised goose bumps across her skin. Several of the warriors landed awkwardly, then slumped to the sands with limbs bent in ways that even their multi-jointed appendages were meant to contort. The intergalactic tyrant stood angrily in their midst. He hadn't even bothered to draw his sword. His genetic enhancements had saved him from the attack.

Two of the warriors who had dispatched his guards approached cautiously. They wielded four weapons each. Genghis smiled at them as they began circling him. As one, most likely coordinated by their hive queen, the two attacked. Genghis' movements were quicksilver. For nearly a minute, he wove in and out of the insectoids' attacks. None of their blows landed. The two warriors worked in perfect synch, pressing their attack. The Khan wasn't even breathing hard as he caught the first sword. A loud crack rang out into the desert as he shattered it, then spun away to dodge the next strikes.

Watching the beautiful, deadly dance unfold as more warriors regained their feet, Dracanna began to see the depth that Genghis Khan had gone to in order to make himself more than just immortal. He was nigh unstoppable.

***

"We're here to rescue you," Thorial Five said, rushing to the cage. In his hurry he tilted his head and his dark wig slid off and landed unnoticed at his feet.

"You fool, I'm beyond rescue," she murmured.

"What do you mean?" He grabbed hold of the golden bars, then screamed. Electricity danced over the cage, sending massive current through the Gray. He shook and screamed as the power assaulted him. The reek of roasting flesh filled the room while the sizzle reverberated around them. The whole cage glowed and sparked, but Meridia didn't move.

"Somebody do something!" Conrad shouted.

"Too much power," one of the other Grays said.

"We can never get close to it!" another shouted, dropping the wicker basket it carried.

"Sassy, I think we need some help here!" Conrad called into the small communications button they'd sewn into the top of his blouse.

"Why don't we just pull the plug?" Bea asked, walking over a cord that ran from the cage into the heavy rugs that covered the floor. She pulled out her small blaster and fired. A beam of red light burned through the cord. The sparks stopped and Thorial dropped to the floor, his hands still burning.

"Here." One of the other Grays pulled off its blouse to smother the flames.

Meridia cried louder, then another wail joined hers.

"What's going on here?" Sassy stepped out of the shadows.

The imprisoned alien turned toward them. A small pink baby with large brown eyes and black hair rested in her arms.

***

As Genghis spun to remove a sword from his other opponent, more sand erupted a few feet from them. Even though she turned, some of the sand still managed to find its way into Dracanna's face. Her eyes watered as she blinked furiously to clear them.

"Your reign on my world is over, little man!" clicked a powerful voice. An Insectoid Queen stood there before them. More warriors swarmed around her, making a living shield between her and their Mongolian overlord. Somewhere nearby shouts went up, calling for guards to protect the Khan.

"Don't flatter yourself, Queenie," Genghis said, speaking for the first time since the attack began. "I can hold my own against you and every bug on *my* world. Do you think I'd be so foolish as to come out here with only two guards and Dracanna if I couldn't handle anything you rebels tried to throw at me?" He drove a wave of mental power at the queen.

Its energy sang in Dracanna's mind.

The queen's warriors moved to intercept it. It flung them to the side, shattering many of them on the sand.

Wave upon wave of insectoid warriors flung themselves up to protect their queen. Some of them darted forward to assault the Khan, but he thrust them away with his mind. Dracanna had never seen such force before. She knew there were several races in the known universe that could use their minds as weapons, but none of them possessed this level of power. *He must've found a way to amplify the power he had access to. If this revolt is going to work,* I *have to think of a way to stop him.*

***

"Whoa, where did the baby come from?" Bea slipped her blaster back into her purse. To Conrad, she looked overly calm. The alien baby was one of the strangest things he'd ever seen. From one angle it looked like a normal dark-haired baby. From another, its huge eyes and pointed chin looked way too much like a Gray to naturally have hair. And its crying, every time it wailed, a pain shot through the back of his eyes. *What's with that?*

"It is mine," Meridia wailed. "Genghis wished to see if he could impregnate me. Now we have a child."

"That is *not* possible!" Thorial Five roared.

"Apparently it is," Sassy said. Conrad stepped out of the way allowing him to pass. The Sasquatch strolled over and bent a bar away from the locking door of the cage. "We've known for a while that he was pushing his genetic manipulation plans along with his knowledge of magic. He must've found some way to do more than steal Gray DNA from Meridia, he must've forced her to carry a baby too."

"But I was supposed to be the one to carry *our* child!" Thorial screamed. He turned and ran from the room. Travis started after him, but Conrad shook his head. *We'll catch up to him.*

Bea reached into the cage for the Gray and her child. "Look, regardless of all this, sweetie, we need to get you out of here and off this world."

"I didn't think Dracanna got involved in people's

174

problems," the crying mother sniffled as she moved toward Bea's hands.

"Sometimes, even the Scary Queen herself can rise to the occasion," Bea replied with a chuckle. "She's the one who led Genghis away so we could come get you. Now let's get out of here before someone gets suspicious."

"I can get them out the fastest," Sassy said. "They're small enough I can carry them through the shadows and meet you back at Shoppe. My people are readied there to swarm the city if we need to."

"I hope it won't come to that," Conrad said. Like so many plans, this one was changing by the second. They'd planned on getting into the yurt while Dracanna lead Genghis into the Insectoid trap, smuggle Meridia out in one of the baskets, then get back to Shoppe and if necessary send people out to help stop Genghis. It was the last part of the plan he didn't like.

Sassy helped Bea assist Meridia free of the cage, then the big biped snapped the golden collar that rested around the alien's neck. There was no loud noise, no flying fragments. The collar just broke like chilled taffy in the huge hairy hands.

Meridia reached up with her free hand and rubbed her neck where the collar had rested. New tears ran down her pale face. "It has been so long."

"You there, halt!" A loud Mongolian voice rang out from the other room.

Conrad spotted the fallen wig and realized that Thorial was in trouble.

***

With all of the hives of the world behind her, the Insectoid queen might be able to fend off Genghis's mental attacks, but Dracanna doubted she was making any progress in attacking the warlord. *I didn't want to get my nails bloodied in this, but I might have to.*

The queen drew herself up to her full height, nearly twelve feet tall. The pinchers on her arms were barren of weapons, but if she could successfully bring them to bear against the Kahn, then she might just be able to do some damage. But the way he was hurling her warriors about with his mental attacks, the odds of that were slim. Behind them, more shouts rang out. Pretty soon, more soldiers would be there. *It's time to act.*

Flowing up behind Genghis, Dracanna moved undetected. She grabbed hold of his shoulder. He turned toward her and started to say something, but she slammed her fist into his face with all her strength. His head twisted away from her. With lightning fast speed, she extended her fangs and buried them in his neck.

The Khan struggled. A scream escaped his lips, but he couldn't dislodge the feeding vampire from his throat. *He must not know that there is no way, outside of death, to dislodge a feeding vampire, once it has begun to suck blood. That's one of the biggest secrets on Darkholme. My family would never let that one out.* His blood washed past her tongue. A surge of power passed through Dracanna. The life she drained from him was sweeter and stronger than any she'd ever tasted before. With each genetically-enhanced drop, she knew which species he'd gotten DNA from. She'd met most of them, and heard of a few others, but there were a couple that even she'd never heard of before. *How did he retain his human form?* With all the aliens spliced into his genetic code, it seemed impossible.

"Stop, Dracanna!" he shouted in her mind.

"No, Genghis," she replied, not loosening her bite. His blood tasted so good. *"Your reign has gone on long*

enough. Look at what you have done to yourself. You're not even close to human any more. It's time to free the universe from your grasp."

He clawed at her arm, but didn't faze her. *"But I thought you were a friend."*

"Genghis, friends don't try and steal each other's secrets. You were a customer, nothing more, nothing less. We walked around each other with careful steps for over a thousand years, like two old, weary tigers." Under her lips, his pulse began to fade.

Arms pulled at her from behind, but she had temporarily absorbed much of Genghis by drinking his blood. She thrust out a hand, and mental force rolled the unseen Mongolian away from her.

"You realize this won't be the end of my empire!" he said weakly.

"Right now I don't care," she replied mentally, refusing to let go of him until she'd finished every last drop. *"I stopped caring when you turned out to be tastier than some of my best ice cream."*

***

"Sassy, get her out of here!" Conrad shouted. "We'll meet you back at Shoppe. If your people want to storm the city, let them." As the Sasquatch scooped up the Gray and her child, he pulled out the mini blaster that Bea had given him before they set out. "The rest of you, let's go rescue Thorial and do what we can to cause chaos on the way back to Shoppe."

Travis grabbed his arm as they turned toward the curtain leading to the yurt's main room. "You know, this was more fun that I would've thought. I've got your back, but don't do anything stupid."

Conrad gave him a quick kiss. "You don't do

anything stupid either. We've got some better fun to have once this is all over." Holding Travis's hand, he pushed through the curtain into the dining room.

A guard pulled a long curved sword out of Thorial's body, letting the Gray slide to the floor with a heavy thud. With a glare, followed closely by a wild war cry, the guard charged toward them. He skidded to a stop halfway across the room, turned and ran toward the entrance flap.

With heavy hands, Conrad aimed the blaster at the fleeing guard and shot him in the back. Before the man fell to the floor, the flap swung aside and two more guards ran in, swords out.

Bea's blaster fire buzzed through the air past Conrad's head as he took aim. The guard on the left swung his shiny blade at the oncoming beam of light. The two met just right for the sword to deflect the blaster's beam. The ricocheted bolt burned a hole through the thick hide of the yurt's wall. A thin wisp of rancid smoke wafted up from the hole.

"I hate it when they bring bright swords to a blaster fight!" Bea shouted as Conrad fired his weapon again.

The guard to the right deflected his beam. "I agree Bea!"

"These guards are some of the best in the known universe, honey," she replied. "I hope we don't end up going man to man with them."

"I got no problem with that," Travis said. "Conrad, when I grab the sword, you shoot the bastard." He charged forward, followed by two of the Grays swinging their wicker baskets high.

"Travis, wait!" Conrad shouted, but he was already in motion. All Conrad could do was watch and aim. Travis attacked the closest guard with his mop. The sharp steel sword clanged against the fiberglass handle. The guard twisted to meet Travis' attack. Conrad got the opening he needed to fire. The Mongolian punched the cowboy hard in the face. Travis tumbled over backward. Conrad fired the blaster at the side of the man's head. The beam split the iron-covered skull with deadly accuracy Conrad had never had when firing guns in the military.

Not waiting to see how Bea dealt with the second guard, he raced to Travis' side. Travis tried to sit up. His blue eyes were hazy and unfocused. A large dark bruise was already forming along the ridge of his nose and going up onto his forehead.

"What happened to not doing anything stupid?" Conrad asked, taking the man's face in his hands. His heart beat faster. The adrenaline from the fight merged with the flood of emotions from seeing Travis hurt. New feeling surged up in him.

One of the Grays flew past him, its head partially cleaved in. Conrad released Travis for a second and picked up the blaster from where it had fallen from his hand. "Crossfire!" he shouted, hoping Bea would understand. She nodded. He fired. She fired. The guard wasn't able to defend against beams from two directions at once. He caught Conrad's beam, but Bea's blew a hole right through the center of his chest.

Conrad turned his attention back to Travis. "Now what was this about not doing anything stupid?"

Travis smiled. "It worked, didn't it?"

"Yeah it worked, but we still have to get through the streets back to Shoppe before this is all over."

"And we need to get moving," Bea said. The remaining Grays all scattered through the yurt flap.

Offering Travis a hand up, Conrad couldn't help but smile. They'd managed to free Meridia. Thorial was dead, but he might not have been if he hadn't freaked out and run off without his wig. They had no way of knowing what was happening with Dracanna and Genghis, but that wasn't their part of the plan. It was up to the Insectoid queen to finish off the Mongolian dictator. It was her world. With luck they'd be leaving it soon enough. He kissed Travis again as they started out the flap for their trip back to Shoppe.

***

Dracanna straightened and wiped the last trickle of blood from her lips as the lifeless form that had been Genghis Khan dropped from her grasp onto the dusty desert sands. The Insectoid queen stared, her multi-faceted eyes unreadable. The people of Genghis lined up behind to watch in stunned silence.

"You have robbed me of my victory," the insect queen said quietly.

With a heavy, contented sigh, Dracanna said, "I believe I just handed you your victory. Genghis Khan is dead. The planet is yours to do with as you please. Show mercy to his people, allow them to leave so you may rebuild your people and culture as you and the other hive queens see fit. I'm sure there are other places in the universe they can go and be welcome."

"But you are the one who defeated the tyrant," the queen objected. Her warriors parted as she stepped closer to Dracanna, lowering herself to be on eye level. "It is now your planet."

"I don't want this planet, or anything else Genghis had. I want all of you to go back to the lives you had before he appeared. I realize you're young. Is there not an older hive queen that can help you remake this world into its former glory?"

The giant bug shook her head. "No. Of the queens that

now rule in secret, I am the oldest and my warriors are the strongest."

Dracanna reached out and patted the Insectoid on the head. "Then make of this what you will. It's your opportunity to shape a world. Do a good job of it." It had been a long time since she'd had a hand in overthrowing a regime. Like the last time, she didn't plan on sticking around to watch how it played out. She had Shoppe, and the freedom to move about as she wanted, bringing tasty treats to a hard stale universe that needed them.

With sand trickling into her black heels, Dracanna turned away from the Insectoids and the body of the former Mongolian despot. She wanted to get back into space, where she belonged.

***

More guards ran toward them as Conrad, Bea and Travis fought their way out of the area around Genghis's yurt. Luckily they weren't all as good with their swords as the ones stationed at the flap of the tent had been. Conrad and Bea were able to shoot most of them until their blasters began to run low.

"Damn," Bea said. "I knew this was going too easy."

"Now what?" Travis asked.

Conrad glanced around as four guards closed in around them. Several more lay dead closer to them. "Grab swords. We may not be as good as they are with them, but we have to at least try."

"Speak for yourself, honey," Bea said. "I've been with the scary bitch long enough to pick up a bit of sword play…with steel. I was good with the flesh kind long before I met her." She dove for a sword, rolled and came up in a crouch, her skirt spread wide before the next guard. She swung the sword upwards, catching him between the legs and pulling it out from his stomach.

Conrad ran to the closest sword. He managed to get it up as a guard rushed him. The two sharp pieces of steel meeting sent shockwaves down his arms. It pushed him back a step. He tried to remember all the swordplay he'd seen before. *Form doesn't matter. The important thing is getting the sword into the flesh of the opponent.* As he swung, he stilled his mind, like he did when he shot a gun. Like a baseball bat, the sword became an extension of his arm. He thrust forward. The guard blocked him. Again, the shock of the two swords connecting vibrated through his body. Then he was forced to arc the sword down and block a blow. Watching his opponent, he noticed the way the man moved like a dancer. If he watched each movement, he began to know what the next movement was going to be. Even without the loud disco music from the clubs that surrounded the ice cream shop back in Dallas, he fell into a dance mode. A swing, a block, a swish and repeat. The clang of their steel rang out. He started working out in his mind what the guard's movements were going to be. *I have to think fast. To win and survive, I have to take control of this deadly dance. Unfortunately, I've always been the type to let the other man lead.*

He stumbled. His foot caught on the hem of his long woolen skirt. The guard's sword tip caught his cheek. Fire blazed across his face. *Enough with the girl's clothes!* Conrad ripped the button off the front as he brought his sword up one-handed to block. He then whipped the skirt from around his waist and flung it in the guard's face. The man backed up, trying to free himself of the covering cloth. Returning two hands to the sword's hilt, Conrad cleaved downward with all his might. Sharp steel shredded the skirt and caught the guard in the shoulder. The sword tore through the leather armor protecting the guard and stopped against his collar bone.

A muffled scream came from the guard as he reeled backward. Conrad pressed the attack. He didn't know how many of the Mongolians he'd already killed with the blaster. There was something more satisfying about doing it up close with the sword. With a final horizontal swing, he managed to separate the man's head from his neck.

Chest heaving and blood dripping down his face, Conrad paused and looked around. Bea easily backed up her opponent, forcing the short man down a side path, dust blowing up around them with every step. But Travis wasn't doing so well. A tall guard pressed him back into the cloth wall of a yurt. Sweat glistened on Travis' pale face as the guard raised his sword to bring it down. Conrad knew he couldn't get across the dusty path in time to save the cowboy. He pulled his blaster back out and threw the small weapon.

"Hey you!" he shouted as the blaster bounced off the man's helmet.

The guard paused long enough for Travis to roll out of the way.

"AAAARRRRRRR!" Conrad screamed as he held the sword in front of him and charged. The guard turned from Travis and took up a stance to block Conrad's assault. Swinging with all his might, he forced the guard back. A glint of metal flashed behind the guard. Then a moment later, the tip of Travis's sword emerged from the guard's chest even as Conrad blocked the man's attack. The guard staggered. Conrad sidestepped and let him fall to the ground. The sword was buried halfway through the man's body.

"Genghis Kahn is dead!" someone screamed nearby.

Conrad didn't care, he gathered Travis up in his arms

and kissed him. The sweat and blood added a salty taste to his lips and the scruff of the man's blond goatee felt good.

"You okay?" he asked as their lips parted.

"I think so," Travis replied. "But you're bleeding."

"We'll look at that when we get back to Shoppe," Bea said. She wiped her sword clean on the edge of her skirt. "My guy just took off. If Genghis is dead, this whole area is about to erupt into chaos. Let's go home."

"Good idea," Conrad said, keeping a firm grip on his sword with his right hand, while holding onto Travis' hand with the left.

8
The Last Bite

Dracanna stared at the new raspberry crème table. From what she could tell, it was perfect. She had thought about finding a way to get the craftsman and his equipment into Shoppe so that she'd always have access to spare tables. But there were other people in the universe that could make what she needed. She'd managed to get the ones he'd been making for Genghis from him, so she had spares as long as a catastrophe didn't strike again and break them. It hadn't taken any effort to also get the spirit jar. That was something that she didn't want to get into the shaman's hands.

She looked around her store. Everything was in order. All the tables and chairs were where they belonged. All the ice cream tubs were in their proper spots in the freezer. Over the past two days, they'd even managed to get the place spotless. It looked like she was ready to open for business, but it was time to take off and she couldn't wait to get free of the miserable desert world.

Most of the non-native species were leaving Mongoleon. The Insectoid queen couldn't even remember what the world had been called before Genghis took it over and she hadn't thought of a new name for the place. The uneasy truce she had with the Grays was the first thing she dissolved. She'd thanked them politely for their help and ordered them back into space. Since it had been Gray tech that caused all the problems in the first place, the Grays, along with Sassy's people, offered to help get the Mongolians off world because their ships were all out preparing for an attack on Darkholme. Dracanna shivered. It would be a while before she forgot the sight of Archon Khan's face when she and the Gray commander informed the youngest of Genghis's adult children of his father's demise and the loss of his homeworld. The man was still set on conquering Darkholme and making a new homeworld for the Mongolians, all in his father's name. Like it or not, she knew her battles were just beginning.

"Scoop, get everyone up here," she said. "It's time to take off."

***

Conrad yawned and rolled over to look at Travis. The blond man sprawled sleepily in the bed they'd been given in the crew quarters, which it turned out, were behind the store room. They'd had a quiet night, but then they had to after Bea complained about the noise they'd made their first night together. Conrad still didn't know if it was after combat energy or just Travis' skills, but it was a night he was going to remember for a very long time. Behind Travis, the only thing they'd put on the wall so far was the swords they'd used in killing the guards. Travis' blade hung across his. He liked the way the weapons looked there.

"Are you sure you don't want her to drop us back on Earth?" Travis said softly, opening his blue eyes to stare up at Conrad.

"Yeah." Conrad nodded. "I'm sure. It may be

strange…okay, downright bizarre, but this feels more right than anything I've done since getting out of the Air Force."

Travis chuckled. "Even with the skirts?"

He frowned and sighed. "Even with the skirts. But are you okay with us staying with Dracanna and the Scary Queen?"

"Hey, I've never been outside Texas. Like you say, it's bizarre, but it's an adventure. Almost like the first time I wandered into a gay bar in Dallas. But then there were people shooting guns, not swinging swords. Besides, you're a cool guy, Conrad Bale. I like it when you get all butch and save me." He leaned up and kissed Conrad. "I'd like to get to know you better."

Warmth flooded through Conrad. He'd admired Travis from afar before their adventure began, now he got to experience the cowboy the way he'd always dreamed. It was something he wanted to keep doing.

Smiling, he kissed the man again. "I want to get to know you better, too."

"All hands to the serving counter," Scoop's voice rang out over the intercom.

"I guess we're about ready to head out," Conrad said after another quick kiss before he swung his long legs out of the bed and reached for his jeans and the new lizard skin boots that had been delivered the day before. At least he'd managed to talk Dracanna into only having to wear drag when the shop was open or he was on official business for her.

***

"What's taking them so long?" Dracanna snarled as Bea walked in from the back room.

"Oh sweetie, you know young love, they were up most of the night again, but not nearly as loud as the first night," she replied. "They'll be here in a couple of minutes."

"Do we all have to be here to take off?" Meridia asked, shifting her baby to her other arm. "This ship isn't very efficient if it can't take off without the whole crew on the bridge."

"It's not a bridge, and no, the whole crew doesn't have to be here, but I want them here," Dracanna snapped. "They need to see how this works when things go smoothly. The flight here was less than stellar."

"Very well," the Gray replied. "I want to thank you again for taking me and little Thorial in. I was tempted to run both of us through with a sword. You have no idea the shame I have endured. I would have no right to ask my people to take me in after everything that I have done." The woman had been thanking Dracanna since she agreed to let the Gray be the dishwasher and work in the backroom for support of her and her baby. The child was obviously Genghis', but how many of his strange genetic traits he'd passed on to it had still not been determined and probably wouldn't be for many years. *It makes sense to keep it close, where I can watch it and help shape it. Being half Gray, we aren't even sure what sex it is yet.*

"After years of being imprisoned, you deserve more than dead," Dracanna said. "Now, just don't prove me wrong."

The door swung open and Conrad and Travis strolled in. The two men had silly contented looks on their faces. Shoppe had felt happy when Conrad announced that he was going to stay as part of her crew. She still hadn't told anyone, not even Scoop, why she liked the man so much. But having him there and happy gave her an extra sparkle in the tile floors and metal rail running behind the cash register.

"Good we're all here." Dracanna announced. "I hope

you two slept well."

Conrad nodded. "We did, thanks."

"Scoop, is Pal in sync with Shoppe?" she asked as she strolled over to the ice cream freezer and motioned across the glass to activate the control panel.

"He is," Scoop replied from his rack next to the cash register. "They both assure me that there won't be any trouble making the jump to Darkholme."

"Good." She poised her talon-like fingers over the controls. "Well Conrad, Travis and Meridia, as this is the first time you have ever experienced a *planned* departure in the Scary Queen, I need to wish you all safe journeys in the spaceways, and tasty treats along the way. This should go much smoother than the previous flight."

"I hope so," Conrad said, reaching out to take Travis's hand.

Dracanna's fingers flew over the controls, setting the course that she'd promised herself over a thousand years earlier that she'd never take. Shoppe shook slightly. The lights dimmed and brightened and they were underway.

"Next stop, Darkholme," she said as a feeling of dread settled into her chest.

The End.

Stay tuned for Tales of the Scary Queen Volume 2

A.M. Burns currently lives in the beautiful Colorado mountains surrounded by nature, his loving partner, several dogs, a couple of cats, some horses, and a red tailed hawk. When not hard at work on his next writing project he spends time out photographing the magical world around him.

Learn More about A.M. and keep up to date on his projects
at
www.amburns.com